'What do you think would happen if we followed through on this?'

Her skin sizzled where his hand lay on her arm. She could feel the graze of the rough callus on his fingers, reminding her that he was a man in every sense of the word. 'Um... I'm not sure what you mean. Follow through on what?'

His eyes searched hers for a lengthy moment. 'So that's the way you're going to play it. Ignore it. Pretend it's not there.'

He gave a little laugh that sounded very deep and very sexy.

'That could work.'

Izzy pressed her lips together, trying to summon up some will-power. Where had it gone? Had she left it behind in England? It certainly wasn't here with her now. 'I think it's for the best, don't you?'

'You reckon you've got what it takes to unlock this banged-up cynical heart of mine, Dr Courtney?'

He was mocking her again. She could see it in the way the corner of his mouth was tilted and his eyes glinted at her in the darkness.

She gave him a pert look to disguise how tempted she was to take him on. 'I'm guessing I'd need a lot more than a month—that is if I could be bothered, which I can't.'

He brushed an idle fingertip underneath the base of her upraised chin. 'I would like nothing better right now than to take you inside and show you a good time.'

Izzy suppressed the shiver of longing his light touch evoked.

Dear Reader

I love fish-out-of-water stories, where a character—usually the heroine!—is thrown into a situation or environment that is totally foreign to her. Like me right now! I am writing this on a four-wheel drive tour bus in The Kimberleys in Western Australia. The heat is intense, but the scenery and the small friendly communities we've travelled through are wonderful examples of the wild frontier of the Outback and the larger-than-life people who make it so special.

Lady Isabella (Izzy) Courtney has taken a four-week posting to Jerringa Ridge after the end of her four-year engagement. She's not looking for love, but Cupid has other plans.

Sergeant Zach Fletcher is the local cop, who also has a broken relationship behind him and has no interest in anything right now but helping his dad get back on his feet after a quad bike accident. But of course when Zach meets Izzy everything changes—for both of them.

They both learn—as I too have learnt over the years—that it doesn't matter where you live, as long as the one you love is with you.

I hope you enjoy Zach and Izzy's story.

Warmest wishes

Melanie Milburne

FLIRTING WITH THE WITH THE SOCIALITE DOC

BY
MELANIE MILBURNE

Published in Great Britain 2014
by Mills & Boon, an imprint of Harlequin (UK) Limited,
Eton House, 18-24 Paradise Road, Richmond, Surrey, TW9 1SR

© 2014 Melanie Milburne

ISBN: 978 0 263 24372 7

Harlequin (UK) Limited's policy is to use papers that are natural,
renewable and recyclable products and made from wood grown in
sustainable forests. The logging and manufacturing processes conform
to the leg

Printed at
by CPI A

From as soon as **Melanie Milburne** could pick up a pen she knew she wanted to write. It was when she picked up her first Mills & Boon® at seventeen that she realised she wanted to write romance. After being distracted for a few years by meeting and marrying her own handsome hero, surgeon husband Steve, and having two boys, plus completing a Masters of Education and becoming a nationally ranked athlete (masters swimming), she decided to write. Five submissions later she sold her first book and is now a multi-published, bestselling, award-winning *USA Today* author. In 2008 she won the Australian Readers' Association most popular category/ series romance, and in 2011 she won the prestigious Romance Writers of Australia R*BY award.

Melanie loves to hear from her readers via her website, www.melaniemilburne.com.au, or on Facebook: www.facebook.com/melanie.milburne

Recent titles by Melanie Milburne:

DR CHANDLER'S SLEEPING BEAUTY
SYDNEY HARBOUR HOSPITAL: LEXI'S SECRET*
THE SURGEON SHE NEVER FORGOT
THE MAN WITH THE LOCKED AWAY HEART

Sydney Harbour Hospital

These books are also available in eBook format from www.millsandboon.co.uk

CHAPTER ONE

EVEN THE DISTANCE of more than seventeen thousand kilometres that Izzy had put between herself and her best friend was not going to stop another Embarrassing Birthday Episode from occurring.

Oh, joy.

'I've got the perfect present winging its way to you,' Hannah crowed over the phone from London. 'You're going to get the biggest surprise. Be prepared. Be very prepared.'

Izzy gave a mental groan. Her closest friend from medical school had a rather annoying habit of choosing the most inappropriate and, on occasion, excruciatingly embarrassing birthday gifts. 'I know you think I'm an uptight prude but do you have to rub my nose in it every year? I'm still blushing from that grotesque sex toy you gave me last year.'

Hannah laughed. 'This is so much better. And it will make you feel a little less lonely. So how are you settling in? What's it like out there?'

'Out there' was Jerringa Ridge and about as far away from Izzy's life back in England as it could be, hot and dry with sunlight that wasn't just bright but violent. Unlike other parts of New South Wales, which had suffered unusually high levels of flooding, it hadn't rained, or at least with any significance, in this district for months.

And it looked like it.

A rust-red dust cloud had followed her into town like a dervish and left a fine layer over her car, her clothes, and had somehow even got into the small cottage she'd been assigned for her four-week locum.

'It's hot. I swear I got sunburnt walking from the car to the front door.' Izzy glanced down at the tiny white circle on her finger where her engagement ring had been for the last four years. *Not sunburnt enough.*

'Have you met any of the locals yet?'

'Just a couple of people so far,' Izzy said. 'The clinic receptionist, Margie Green, seems very nice, very motherly. She made sure the cottage was all set up for me with the basics. There's a general store run by a husband and wife team—Jim and Meg Collis—who are very friendly too. And the guy who owns and operates the local pub—I think his name is Mike something or other—has organised a welcome-drink-cum-party for me for tomorrow night. Apparently the locals grab at any excuse to party so I didn't like to say I'd prefer to lie low and find my feet first.'

'Perfect timing,' Hannah said. 'At least you won't be on your own on your birthday.'

On your own...

Izzy was still getting used to being single. She'd become so used to fitting in with Richard Remington's life—*his meticulously planned life*—that it was taking her a little while to adjust. The irony was she had been the one to end things. Not that he'd been completely devastated or anything. He'd moved on astonishingly quickly and was now living with a girl ten years younger than he was who had been casually employed to hand around drinks at one of his parents' soirees—another irony, as he had been so adamant about not moving in with Izzy while they'd been together.

This four weeks out at Jerringa Ridge—the first of six one-month locums she had organised in Australia—would give her the space to stretch her cramped wings, to finally fly free from the trappings and expectations of her aristocratic background.

Out here she wasn't Lady Isabella Courtney with a pedigree that went back hundreds of years.

She was just another GP, doing her bit for the Outback.

'Have you met the new doctor yet?' Jim Collis asked, as Zach Fletcher came into the general store to pick up some supplies the following day.

'Not yet.' Zach picked up a carton of milk and checked the use-by date. 'What's he like?'

'She.'

He turned from the refrigerated compartment with raised brows. 'No kidding?'

'You got something against women doctors?' Jim asked.

'Of course not. I just thought a guy had taken the post. I'm sure that's what William Sawyer said before he went on leave.'

'Yeah, well, it seems that one fell through,' Jim said. 'Dr Courtney stepped into the breach at the last minute. She's from England. Got an accent like cut glass.'

Zach grunted as he reached for his wallet. 'Hope she knows what she's in for.'

Jim took the money and put it in the till. 'Mike's putting on a welcome do for her tonight at the pub. You coming?'

'I'm on duty.'

'Doesn't mean you can't pop in and say g'day.'

'I'd hate to spoil the party by showing up in uniform,' Zach said.

'I don't know…' Jim gave him a crooked grin. 'Some women really get off on a guy in uniform. You could get lucky, Fletch. Be about time. How long's it been?'

Zach gave him a look as he stuffed his wallet in his back pocket. 'Not interested.'

'You're starting to sound like your old man,' Jim said. 'How is he? You haven't brought him into town for a while.'

'He's doing OK.'

Jim gave him a searching look. 'Sure?'

Zach steeled his gaze. 'Sure.'

'Tell him we're thinking of him.'

'Will do.' Zach turned to leave.

'Her name is Isabella Courtney,' Jim said. 'Got a nice figure on her and pretty too, in a girl-next-door sort of way.'

'Give it a break, Jim.'

'I'm just saying…'

'The tyres on your ute are bald.' Zach gave him another hardened look as he shouldered open the door. 'Change them or I'll book you.'

Zach's father Doug was sitting out on the veranda of Fletcher Downs homestead; the walking frame that had been his constant companion for the last eighteen months by his side. A quad-bike accident had left Doug Fletcher with limited use of his legs. It would have been a disaster for any person, but for a man who only knew how to work and live on the land it was devastating.

Seeing his strong and extremely physically active father struck down in such a way had been bad enough, but the last couple of months his dad had slipped into a funk of depression that made every day a nightmare of anguish for Zach. Every time he drove up the long drive to the homestead his heart rate would escalate in panic in case his dad had done something drastic in his absence, and it wouldn't slow down again until he knew his father had managed to drag himself through another day.

Popeye, the toy poodle, left his father's side to greet Zach with a volley of excited yapping. In spite of everything, he couldn't help smiling at the little mutt. 'Hey, little buddy.' He crouched down and tickled the little dog's soot-black fleecy ears. He'd chosen the dog at a rescue shelter in Sydney when he'd gone to bring his dad home from the rehabilitation centre. Well, really, it had been the other way around. Popeye had chosen him. Zach had intended to get a man's dog, a kelpie or a collie, maybe even a German shepherd like the one he'd worked with in the drug squad, but somehow the little black button eyes had looked at him unblinkingly as if to say, *Pick me!*

'Jim says hello,' Zach said to his father as he stepped into the shade of the veranda.

His father acknowledged the comment with a grunt as he continued to stare out at the parched paddocks, which instead of being lime green with fresh growth were the depressing colour of overripe pears.

'There's a new doctor in town—a woman.' Zach idly kicked a stray pebble off the floorboards of the veranda into the makeshift garden below. It had been a long time since flowers had grown there. Twenty-three years, to be exact. His English born and bred mother had attempted to grow a cottage garden similar to the one she had left behind on her family's country estate in Surrey, but, like her, none of the plants had flourished in the harsh conditions of the Outback.

'You met her?' His father's tone was flat, as if he didn't care one way or the other, but at least he had responded. That meant it was a good day. A better day.

'Not yet,' Zach said. 'I'm on duty this evening. I'm covering for Rob. I thought I'd ask Margie to come over and sit with—'

Doug's mouth flattened. 'How many times do I have to tell you I don't need a bloody babysitter?'

'You hardly see any of your old mates these days. Surely a quiet drink with—'

'I don't want people crying and wringing their hands and feeling sorry for me.' Doug pulled himself to his feet and reached for his walker. 'I'll see people when I can drive into town and walk into the pub on my own.'

Zach watched as his father shuffled back down the other end of the veranda to the French doors that led to his bedroom. The lace curtains billowed out like a ghostly wraith as the hot, dry northerly wind came through, before the doors closed with a rattling snap that made every weatherboard on the old house creak in protest.

These days it seemed every conversation he had with his dad ended in an argument. Moving back home after five years of living in the city had seemed the right idea at the time, but now he wondered if it had made things worse. It had changed their relationship too much. He'd always planned to come back to the country and run Fletcher Downs once his father was ready to retire, but the accident had thrown everything out of order. This far out in the bush it was hard to get carers to visit, let alone move in, and without daily support his father would have no choice but to move off the property that had been in the family for seven generations.

The day Zach's mother had left had broken his father's heart; leaving Fletcher Downs before his time would rip it right out of his chest.

Popeye gave a little whine at Zach's feet. He bent back down and the dog leapt up into his arms and proceeded to anoint his face with a frenzy of enthusiastic licks. He hugged the dog against his chest as he looked at the sunburnt paddocks. 'We'll get him through this, Popeye. I swear to God we will.'

The Drover's Rest was nothing like the pubs at home but the warm welcome Izzy received more than made up for it. Mike Grantham, the proprietor, made sure she had a drink in her hand and then introduced her to everyone who came in the door. She had trouble remembering all of their names, but she was sure it wouldn't be too long before she got to know them, as she was the only doctor serving the area, which encompassed over two hundred and fifty square kilometres.

Once everyone was inside the main room of the pub Mike tapped on a glass to get everyone's attention. 'A little bird told me it's Dr Courtney's birthday today, so let's give her a big Jerringa Ridge welcome.'

The room erupted into applause and a loud and slightly off-key singing of 'Happy Birthday' as two of the local ladies came out with a cake they had made, complete with candles and Izzy's name piped in icing over the top.

'How did you know it was my birthday?' Izzy asked Mike, once she'd blown out the candles.

'I got a call yesterday,' he said. 'A friend of yours from the old country. She gave me the heads up. Said she had a surprise lined up. It should be here any minute now. Why don't you go and wait by the door? Hey, clear a pathway! Let the doc get through.'

Izzy felt her face grow warm as she made her way through the smiling crowd of locals to the front door of the pub. *Why couldn't Hannah send her flowers or chocolate or champagne, like normal people did?*

And then she saw it.

Not it—*him.*

Tall. Muscled. Toned. Buffed. Clean-shaven. A jaw strong and square and determined enough to land a fighter jet on. A don't-mess-with-me air that was like an invisible wall of glass around him. Piercing eyes that dared you to outstare him.

A male stripper.

Dressed as a cop.

I'm going to kill you, Hannah.

Izzy went into damage control. The last thing she wanted was her reputation ruined before she saw her first patient. She could fix this. It would be simple. Just because Hannah had paid the guy—the rather gorgeous hot guy—to come out all this way and strip for her, it didn't mean she had to let him go through with it.

As long as he got his money, right?

'I'm afraid there's been a change of plan,' she said, before the man could put a foot inside the pub. 'I won't be needing your…er…services after all.'

The man—who had rather unusual grey-blue eyes—looked down at her from his far superior height. 'Excuse me?'

Izzy had to speak in a hushed tone as she could feel the crowd starting to gather behind her. 'Please, will you just leave? I don't want you here. It will spoil everything for me.'

One of the man's eyebrows lifted quizzically. 'Let me get this straight…you don't want me to step inside the pub?'

'No. Absolutely not.' Izzy adopted an adamant stance by planting her hands on her hips. 'And I strictly forbid you to remove any of your clothes in my presence. Do you understand?'

Something in those eyes glinted but the rest of his expression was still deadpan. 'How about if I take off my hat?'

She let out a breath and dropped her arms back by her sides, clenching her hands to keep some semblance of control. She *had* to get rid of him. *Now.* 'Are you *listening* to me? I don't want you here.'

'Last time I looked it was a free country.'

Izzy glowered at him. 'Look, I know you get paid to do this sort of stuff, but surely you can do much better? Don't you find this horribly demeaning, strutting around at parties, titillating tipsy women in a leather thong or whatever it is you get down to? Why don't you go out and get a real job?'

'I love my job.' The glint in his eyes made its brief appearance again. 'I've wanted to do it since I was four years old.'

'Then go and do your job someplace else,' she said

from behind gritted teeth. 'If you don't leave right now, I'm going to call the police.'

'He *is* the police,' Mike called out from behind the bar.

CHAPTER TWO

ZACH LOOKED DOWN at the pretty heart-shaped face that was now blushing a fire-engine-red. Her rosebud mouth was hanging open and her toffee-brown eyes were as wide as the satellite dish on the roof of the pub outside. He put out a hand, keeping his cop face on. 'Sergeant Zach Fletcher.'

Her slim hand quivered slightly as it slid into the cage of his. 'H-how do you do? I'm Isabella Courtney...the new locum doctor...in case you haven't already guessed.'

He kept hold of her hand a little longer than he needed to. He couldn't seem to get the message through to his brain to release her. The feel of her satin-soft skin against the roughness of his made something in his groin tighten like an over-tuned guitar string. 'Welcome to Jerringa Ridge.'

'Thank you.' She slipped her hand away and used it to tuck an imaginary strand of hair behind her ear. 'I'm sorry. I expect you think I'm a complete fool but my friend told me she'd organised a surprise and I thought—well, I thought you were the surprise.'

'Sorry to disappoint you.'

'I'm relieved, not disappointed.' She blushed again.

'Quite frankly, I hate surprises. Hannah—that's my friend—thinks it's funny to shock me. Every year she comes up with something outrageous to make my birthday memorable.'

'I guess this will be one you won't forget in a hurry.'

'Yes…' She bit her lip with her small but perfectly aligned white teeth.

'Is there a Dr Courtney around here?' A young man dressed in a courier delivery uniform came towards them from the car park, his work boots crunching on the dusty gravel.

'Um, I'm Dr Courtney.' Isabella's blush had spread down to her décolletage by now, taking Zach's eyes with it. She was of slim build but she had all the right girly bits, a fact his hormones acknowledged with what felt like a stampede racing through his blood.

Cool it, mate.

Not your type.

'I have a package for you,' the delivery guy said. 'I need a signature.'

Zach watched as Isabella signed her name on the electronic pad. She gave the delivery guy a tentative smile as she took the package from him. It was about the size of a shoebox and she held it against her chest like a shield.

'Aren't you going to open it?' Zach asked.

Her cheeks bloomed an even deeper shade of pink. 'I think I'll wait until I'm…until later.'

There was a small silence…apart from the sound of forty or so bodies shuffling and jostling behind them to get a better view.

Zach had lived long enough in Jerringa Ridge to know it wouldn't take much to get the local tongues wagging. Ever since his fiancée Naomi had called off their relationship when he'd moved back home to take care of his father, everyone in town had taken it upon themselves to find him a replacement. He only had to look at a woman once and the gossip would run like a scrub fire. But whether he was in the city or the country, he liked to keep his private life off the grapevine. It meant for a pretty dry social life but he had other concerns right now.

'I'd better head back to the station. I hope you enjoy the rest of your birthday.' He gave Isabella Courtney a brisk impersonal nod while his body thrummed with the memory of her touch. 'Goodnight.'

Izzy watched Zach stride out of the reach of the lights of the pub to where his police vehicle was parked beneath a pendulous willow tree. *Argh!* If only she'd checked the car park before she'd launched into her I-don't-want-you-here speech. How embarrassing! She had just made an utter fool of herself, bad enough in front of *him* but practically the whole town had been watching. Would she ever live it down? Would everyone snigger at her now whenever they saw her?

And how would she face him again?

Oh, he might have kept his face as blank as a mask but she knew he was probably laughing his head off at her behind that stony cop face of his. Would he snigger as well with his mates at how she had mistaken him for a— Oh, it was too *awful* to even think about.

Of course he didn't look anything like a stripper, not that she had seen one in person or anything, only pictures of some well-built guys who worked the show circuit in Vegas. One of the girls she'd shared a flat with in London had hung their risqué calendar on the back of the bathroom door.

Idiot.

Fool.

Imbecile.

How could you possibly think he was—?

'So you've met our gorgeous Zach,' Peggy McLeod, one of the older cattleman's wives, said at Izzy's shoulder, with obvious amusement in her voice.

Izzy turned around and pasted a smile on her face. 'Um, yes… He seems very…um…nice.'

'He's single,' Peggy said. 'His ex-fiancée changed her mind about moving to the bush with him. He and his dad run a big property out of town—Fletcher Downs. Good with his hands, that boy. Knows how to do just about anything. Make someone a fine husband one day.'

'That's…um, nice.'

'His mum was English too, did you know?' Peggy went on, clearly not expecting an answer for she continued without pause. 'Olivia married Doug after a whirlwind courtship but she never could settle to life on the land. She left when Zach was about eight or nine…or was it ten? Yes, it was ten, I remember now. He was in the same class as one of my sister's boys.'

Izzy frowned. 'Left?'

Peggy nodded grimly. 'Yep. Never came back, not even to visit. Zach used to fly over to England for holidays occasionally. Took him ages to settle in, though. Eventually he stopped going. I don't think he's seen his mother in years. Mind you, he's kind of stuck here now since the accident.'

'The accident?'

'Doug Fletcher rolled his quad bike about eighteen

months back. Crushed his spinal cord.' Peggy shook her head sadly. 'A strong, fit man like that not able to walk without a frame. It makes you want to cry, doesn't it?'

'That's very sad.'

'Zach looks after him all by himself,' Peggy said. 'How he does it is anyone's guess. Doug won't hear of having help in. Too proud and stubborn for his own good. Mind you, Zach can be a bit that way too.'

'But surely he can't look after his father indefinitely?' Izzy said. 'What about his own life?'

Peggy's shoulders went up and down. 'Doesn't have one, far as I can see.'

Izzy walked back to her cottage a short time later. The party was continuing without her, which suited her just fine. Everyone was having a field day over her mistaking Zach Fletcher for a stripper. There was only so much ribbing she could take in one sitting. Just as well she was only here for a month. It would be a long time before she would be able to think about the events of tonight without blushing to the roots of her hair.

The police station was a few doors up from the clinic at the south end of the main street. She hadn't noticed it earlier but, then, during the day it looked like any other nondescript cottage. Now that it was fully dark the police sign was illuminated and the four-wheel-drive police vehicle Zach had driven earlier was parked in the driveway beside a spindly peppercorn tree.

As she was about to go past, Zach came out of the building. He had a preoccupied look on his face and almost didn't see her until he got to the car. He blinked and pulled up short, as if she had appeared from nowhere. He tipped his hat, his voice a low, deep burr in the silence of the still night air. 'Dr Courtney.'

'Sergeant Fletcher.' If he was going to be so formal then so was she. Weren't country people supposed to be friendly? If so, he was certainly showing no signs of it.

His tight frown put his features into shadow. 'It's late to be out walking.'

'I like walking.'

'It's not safe to do it on your own.'

'But it's so quiet out here.'

'Doesn't make it safe.' His expression was grimly set. 'You'd be wise to take appropriate measures in future.'

Izzy put her chin up pertly. 'I didn't happen to see a taxi rank anywhere.'

'Do you have a car?'

'Of course.'

'Next time use it or get a lift with one of the locals.' He opened the passenger door of the police vehicle. 'Hop in. I'll run you home.'

Izzy bristled at his brusque manner. 'I would prefer to walk, if you don't mind. It's only a block and I—'

His grey-blue eyes hardened. 'I do mind. Get in. That's an order.'

The air seemed to pulse with invisible energy as those strong eyes held hers. She held his gaze for as long as she dared, but in the end she was the first to back down. Her eyes went to his mouth instead and a frisson of awareness scooted up her spine to tingle each strand of her hair on her scalp. Something shifted in her belly…a turning, a rolling-over sensation, like something stirring after a long hibernation.

His mouth was set tightly, as tight and determined as his jaw, which was in need of a fresh shave. His eyes were fringed with dark lashes, his eyebrows the same rich dark brown as his hair. His skin was deeply tanned and it was that stark contrast with his eyes that was so heart-stopping. Smoky grey one minute, ice-blue the next, the outer rims of his irises outlined in dark blue, as if someone had traced their circumference with a fine felt-tip marker.

Eyes that had seen too much and stored the memories away somewhere deep inside for private reflection…or haunting.

'Fine, I'll get in,' Izzy said with bad grace. 'But you really need to work on your kerb-side manner.'

He gave her an unreadable look as he closed the door with a snap. She watched him stride around to the driver's side, his long legs covering the distance in no time at all. He was two or three inches over six feet and broad shouldered and lean hipped. When he joined her in the car she felt the space shrink alarmingly. She drew herself in tightly, crossing her arms and legs to keep any of her limbs from coming into contact with his powerfully muscled ones.

The silence prickled like static electricity.

'Peggy McLeod told me about your father's accident,' Izzy said as he pulled to the kerb outside her cottage half a minute later. She turned in her seat to look at him. 'I'm sorry. That must be tough on both of you.'

Zach's marble-like expression gave nothing away but she noticed his hands had tightened on the steering-wheel. 'Do you make house calls?'

'I…I guess so. Is that what Dr Sawyer did?'

'Once a week.'

'Then I'll do it too. When would you like me to come?'

Some of the tension seemed to leave his shoulders

but he didn't turn to look at her. 'I'll ring Margie and make an appointment.'

'Fine.'

Another silence.

'Look, about that little mix-up back at the pub—' she began.

'Forget it,' he cut her off. 'I'll wait until you get inside. Lock the door, won't you?'

Izzy frowned. 'You know you're really spooking me with this over-vigilance. Don't you know everyone in a town this size by name?'

'We have drive-throughs who cause trouble from time to time. It's best not to take unnecessary risks.'

'Not everyone is a big bad criminal, Sergeant Fletcher.'

He reached past her to open her door. Izzy sucked in a sharp breath as the iron bar of his arm brushed against her breasts, setting every nerve off like a string of fireworks beneath her skin.

For an infinitesimal moment her gaze meshed with his.

He had tiny blue flecks in that unreadable sea of grey and his pupils were inky-black. He smelt of lemons with a hint of lime and lemongrass and something else… something distinctly, arrantly, unapologetically male.

A sensation like the unfurling petals of a flower brushed lightly over the floor of her belly.

Time froze.

The air tightened. Pulsed. Vibrated.

'Sorry.' He pulled back and fixed his stare forward again, his hands gripping the steering-wheel so tightly his tanned knuckles were bone white.

'No problem.' Izzy's voice came out a little rusty. 'Thanks for the lift.'

He didn't drive off until she had closed the door of the cottage. She leant back against the door and let out a breath she hadn't realised she'd been holding, listening as his car growled away into the night.

'So what did your friend actually send you for your birthday?' Margie Green asked as soon as Izzy arrived at the clinic the next morning.

'I haven't opened it yet.' *Because I stupidly left it in Sergeant Fletcher's car last night.*

Margie's eyes were twinkling. 'What on earth made you think our Zach was a male stripper?'

Izzy cringed all over again. Was every person in town going to do this to her? Remind her of what a silly little idiot she had been? If so, four weeks couldn't go fast enough. 'Because it's exactly the sort of thing my friend Hannah would do. As soon as I saw him standing there I went into panic mode. I didn't stop to think that he could be a real cop. I didn't even know if Jerringa Ridge *had* a cop. I didn't have time to do much research on the post because the agency asked me to step in for someone at the last minute.'

'We have two cops…or one and a half really,' Margie said. 'We used to have four but with all the government cutbacks that's no longer the case. Rob Heywood is close to retirement so Zach does the bulk of the work. He's a hard worker is our Zach. You won't find a nicer man out in these parts.'

'I'm not here to find a man.' Why did every woman over fifty—including her own mother—seem to think younger women had no other goal than to get married? 'I'm here to work.'

Margie cocked her head at a thoughtful angle. 'You're here for four weeks. These days that's a long time for a young healthy woman like you to be without a bit of male company.'

Izzy's left thumb automatically went to her empty ring finger. It was a habit she was finding hard to break. It wasn't that she regretted her decision to end things with Richard. It was just strange to feel so…so unattached. She hadn't looked at another man in years. But now she couldn't get Zach Fletcher's eyes or his inadvertent touch out of her head…*or her body.* Even now she could remember the feel of that slight brush of his arm across her breasts—the electric, tingly feel of hard male against soft female…

She gave herself a mental shake as she picked up a patient's file and leafed through it. 'I'm not interested in a relationship. There'd be no point. I'm on a working holiday. I won't be in one place longer than a month.'

'Zach hasn't dated anyone since he broke up with his ex,' Margie said, as if Izzy hadn't just described her plans for the next six months. 'It'd be good for him to move on. He was pretty cut up about Naomi not wanting to come with him to the bush. Not that he's said anything, of course. He's not one for having his heart flapping about on his sleeve. He comes across as a bit arrogant at times but underneath all that he's a big softie. Mind you, you might have your work cut out for you, being an English girl and all.'

Izzy lowered the notes and frowned. 'Because his mother was English?'

'Not only English but an aristocrat.' Margie gave

a little sniff that spoke volumes. 'One of them blue-blooded types. Her father was a baron or a lord of the realm or some such thing. Olivia Hardwick was as posh as anything. Used to having servants dancing around her all her life. No wonder she had so much trouble adjusting to life out here. Love wasn't enough in the end.'

Izzy thought of the veritable army of servants back at Courtney Manor. They were almost part of the furniture, although she tried never to take any of them for granted. But now was probably not a good time to mention her background with its centuries-old pedigree.

Margie sighed as sat back in her chair. 'It broke Doug's heart when she left. He hasn't looked at another woman since…more's the pity. He and I used to hang out a bit in the old days. Just as friends.'

'But you would have liked something more?' Izzy asked.

Margie gave her a wistful smile. 'We can't always have what we want, can we?'

Izzy glanced at the receptionist's left hand. 'You never married?'

'Divorced. A long time ago. Thirty years this May. I shouldn't have married Jeff but I was lonely at the time.'

'I'm sorry.'

Margie shrugged.

'Did you have children?'

'A boy and a girl. They both live in Sydney. And I have three grandchildren who are the joy of my life. I'm hoping to get down to see them at Easter.'

Izzy wondered if Margie's marriage had come about because of Doug Fletcher's involvement with Olivia. How heartbreaking it must have been for her to watch him fall madly in love with someone else, and how sad for Doug to have the love of his life walk out on him and their young son.

Relationships were tricky. She knew that from her own parents, who had a functional marriage but not a particularly happy or fulfilling one. That was one of the reasons she had decided to end things with Richard. She hadn't wanted to end up trapped in an empty marriage that grumbled on just for the sake of appearances.

'Sergeant Fletcher asked me to make a house call on his father,' Izzy said. 'Has he rung to make an appointment yet?'

'Not yet,' Margie said. 'He might drop in on his way to the station. Ah, here he is now. Morning, Zach. We were just talking about you.'

Izzy turned to see Zach Fletcher duck his head slightly to come through the door. Her stomach did a little freefall as his eyes met hers. He looked incredibly commanding in his uniform; tall and composed with an air of untouchable reserve. How on earth she had mistaken him for anything other than a cop made her cheeks fire up all over again. She ran her tongue over her lips before she gave him a polite but distant smile. 'Good morning, Sergeant Fletcher.'

He dipped his head ever so slightly, his eyes running over her in a lazy, unreadable sweep that set her pulse rate tripping. 'Dr Courtney.'

Izzy's smile started to crack around the edges. Did he have to look at her so unwaveringly, as if he knew how much he unsettled her? Was he laughing at her behind that inscrutable cop mask? 'What can I do for you? Would you like to make an appointment for me to come out and see your father today? I could probably work something in for later this afternoon. I'm pretty solidly booked but—'

He handed her the package the delivery guy had delivered the night before, his eyes locking on hers in a way that made the base of her spine shiver and fizz. 'You left this in my car last night.'

Izzy could practically hear Margie's eyes popping out of her head behind the reception counter. 'Oh... right, thanks.' She took the package from him and held it against her chest, where her heart was doing double time.

'Aren't you going to open it?' Margie said.

'Um...not right now.'

Was that a hint of mockery glinting in Zach Fletcher's eyes? 'What time would suit you?' he asked.

'I...I think I'd rather do it when I get home.'

The glint in his eyes was unmistakable this time, so too was the slight curve at one side of his mouth. His version of a smile? It made her hungry to see a real one. Was he capable of stretching that grim mouth that far? 'I meant what time would suit you to see my father.'

Izzy's blush deepened. What was it about this man that made her feel about twelve years old? Well, maybe not twelve years old. Right now she was feeling *incredibly* adult. X-rated adult. Every particle of her flesh was shockingly aware of him. Her skin was tight, her senses alert, her pulse rate rising, her heart fluttering like a butterfly trapped in the narrow neck of a bottle. 'Oh...' She swung back to Margie. 'What time am I free?'

'Your last patient is at four forty-five. It's a twenty-minute drive out to Fletcher Downs so shall we say five-thirty, give or take a few minutes?' Margie said.

'I'll make sure I'm there to let you in,' Zach said.

'My father can be a bit grouchy meeting people for the first time. Don't let him get to you.'

Izzy raised her chin the tiniest fraction. 'I'm used to handling difficult people.'

His eyes measured hers for a pulsing moment. 'Margie will give you a map. If you pass Blake's waterhole, you've gone too far.'

'I'm sure I'll find it without any trouble,' Izzy said. 'I have satellite navigation in my car.'

He gave a brisk nod that encompassed the receptionist as well as Izzy and left the clinic.

'Are you going to tell me how you ended up in his car last night or am I going to have to guess?' Margie asked.

Izzy let out a breath as she turned back around. 'He gave me a lift home.'

Margie's eyes widened with intrigue. 'From the pub? It's like half a block by city standards.'

'Yes, well, apparently Sergeant Fletcher thinks it's terribly unsafe to walk home at night without an escort. Typical cop, they think everyone's a potential criminal. They never see the good in people, only the bad. They have power issues too. You can pick it up a mile off. I'd bet my bottom dollar Zach Fletcher is a total control freak. And a blind man could see he has a chip on his shoulder the size of a boulder.'

Margie smiled a knowing smile. 'You like him.'

'What on earth gives you that idea?' Izzy gave a scornful little laugh but even to her ears it sounded tinny. 'He's not my type.'

And I bet I'm not his either.

CHAPTER THREE

ZACH HAD BEEN at the homestead long enough to change out of his uniform, make his father a cup of tea, and take Popeye for a walk down to the dam and back when he saw Isabella Courtney coming up the driveway.

He waved a fly away from his face as he watched her handle the corrugations of the gravel driveway that was as long as some city streets. A dust cloud plumed out in her wake and a flock of sulphur-crested white cockatoos and salmon-pink corellas flew out of the gum trees that lined the driveway before settling in another copse of trees closer to the dam. The chorus of cicadas was loud in the oven-warm air and in the distance the grey kangaroo he'd rescued as a joey, and who now had a joey of her own, hopped towards a few tufts of grass that had pushed up through the parched ground around the home paddock's water trough.

Popeye gave a whine and looked up at Zach as his body did its little happy dance at the thought of a visitor. 'Cool it, buddy,' Zach said. 'She's not staying long.'

It was hard to ignore the stirring of male hormones in his body as he watched her alight from the car. She had a natural grace about her, lissom and lithe, like a ballerina or yoga enthusiast. She wasn't particularly tall, or at least not compared to him at six feet three in bare feet. She was about five-six or -seven with a waist he could probably span with his hands, and her features were classically beautiful but in a rather understated way. She wore little or no make-up and her mid-length chestnut hair was tied back in a ponytail she had wound around itself in a casual knot, giving her a fresh, youthful look.

But it was her mouth his gaze kept tracking to. It was soft and full and had an upward curve that made it look like she was always on the brink of smiling.

'Oh, what an adorable dog!' Her smile lit up her brown eyes so much that they sparkled as she bent down to greet Popeye. 'Oh, you darling little poppet. Who's a good boy? Hang on a minute—*are* you a boy? Oh, yes, you are, you sweet little thing. Yes, I love you too.' She laughed a tinkling-bell laugh and stood up again, her smile still stunningly bright as she stood and faced Zach. 'Is he yours?'

Zach had to take a moment to gather himself after being on the receiving end of that dazzling smile.

Earth to Zach. Do you read me?

He wondered if he should fob Popeye off as his father's but he had a feeling she wouldn't buy it for a moment. 'Yes.'

She angled her head at him in an appraising manner. 'Funny, I had you picked as a collie or kelpie man, or maybe a German shepherd or Doberman guy.'

He kept his expression blank. 'The station manager has working dogs. Popeye's just a pet.'

She brushed a tendril of hair away from her face that the light breeze had worked loose. 'This is a lovely property. I couldn't believe how many birds I saw coming up the driveway.'

'You're not seeing it at its best. We need rain.'

She scanned the paddocks with one of her hands shading her eyes against the sun. 'It's still beautiful—Oh, there's a kangaroo and it's got a joey! He just popped his head out. How gorgeous!'

'That's Annie,' Zach said.

She swung around to look at him again. 'Is she a pet too?'

'Not really.' He waved another fly away from his face. 'Her mother was killed on the highway. I reared her by hand and released her back into the wild a few years ago, but she hangs about a bit, mostly because of the drought.'

Her eyes widened in surprise. 'You reared her yourself?'

'Yeah.'

Her pretty little nose was wrinkled over the bridge from her small frown. 'Like with a bottle or something?'

'Yep. Six feeds a day.'

'How did you juggle that with work?'

'I took her with me in a pillowcase.'

She blinked a couple of times as if she couldn't quite imagine him playing wet-nurse. 'That's…amazing…' She looked back at the paddock where Annie was grazing. 'It must be wonderful to have all this space to yourself. To be this close to wildlife and to breathe in such fresh air instead of pollution.'

Zach saw her finely shaped nostrils widen to take in the eucalyptus scent of the bush. He picked up a faint trace of her fragrance in the air: a flowery mix that was redolent of gardenias and vanilla. The sun caught the golden highlights in her hair and he found himself wondering what it would feel like to run his fingers through those glossy, silky strands.

Get a grip.

He thrust his hands in his pockets, out of the way of temptation. She was a blow-in and would be gone before the first dust storm hit town. His track record with keeping women around wasn't flash. His mother had whinged and whined and then withdrawn into herself for ten years before she'd finally bolted and never returned. His fiancée hadn't even got as far as the Outback before the call of the city had drawn her back. Why would Isabella Courtney with her high-class upbringing have anything to offer him?

She turned back to look at him and a slight blush bloomed in her cheeks. 'I guess I should get on with why I came here. Is your father inside?'

'Yes. Come this way.'

Izzy stepped into the cool interior of the homestead but it took her eyes a moment to adjust to the dim interior after the assault of the bright sunlight outside. A man who was an older version of Zach sat in an armchair in the sitting room off the long, wide hallway; a walking frame was positioned nearby. He had steel-grey hair at his temples and his skin was weathered by long periods in the sun but he was still a fine-looking man. He had the same aura of self-containment his son possessed, and a strong uncompromising jaw, although his cheeks were hollowed by recent weight loss. His mouth had a downward turn and his blue eyes had damson-coloured shadows beneath them, as if he had trouble sleeping.

'Dad, Dr Courtney is here,' Zach said.

'Hello, Mr Fletcher.' Izzy held out her hand but dropped it back by her side when Doug Fletcher rudely ignored it.

He turned his steely gaze to his son. 'Why didn't you tell me she was a bloody Pom?'

Zach tightened his mouth. 'Because it has nothing to do with her ability as a medical practitioner.'

'I don't want any toffee-nosed Poms darkening my doorstep ever again. Do you hear me? Get her out of here.'

'Mr Fletcher, I—'

'You need to have regular check-ups and Dr Courtney is the only doctor in the region,' Zach said. 'You either see her or you see no one. I'm not driving three hundred kilometres each way to have your blood pressure checked every week.'

'My blood pressure was fine until you brought her here!' Doug snapped.

Izzy put a hand on Zach's arm. 'It's all right, Sergeant Fletcher. I'll come back some other time.'

Doug glared at her. 'You'll be trespassing if you do.'

'Well, at least the cops won't be far away to charge me, will they?' she said.

Doug's expression was as dark as thunder as he shuffled past them to exit the room. Izzy heard Zach release a long breath and turned to look at him. 'I'm sorry. I don't think I handled that very well.'

He raked a hand through his hair, leaving it sticking up at odd angles. 'You'd think after twenty-three years he'd give it a break, wouldn't you?'

'Is that how long it's been since your mother left?'

He gave her a grim look. 'Yeah. I guess you twigged she was English.'

'Peggy McLeod told me.'

He walked over to the open fireplace and kicked a gum nut back into the grate. His back and shoulders were so tense Izzy could see each muscle outlined by his close-fitting T-shirt. He rubbed the back of his neck before he turned back around to face her. 'I'm worried about him.'

'I can see that.'

'I mean *really* worried.'

Izzy saw the haunted shadows in his eyes. 'You think he's depressed?'

'Let's put it this way, I don't leave him alone for long periods. And I've taken all the guns over to a friend's place.'

She felt her heart tighten at the thought of him having to keep a step ahead of his father all the time. The pressure on the loved ones of people struggling with depression was enormous. And Zach seemed to be doing it solo. 'Has his mood dropped recently or has he been feeling low for a while?'

'It's been going down progressively since he came out of rehab.' He let out another breath as he dragged his hand over his face. 'Each day I seem to lose a little bit more of him.'

Izzy could just imagine the toll it was taking on him. He had so many responsibilities to shoulder, running his father's property as well as his career as a cop. 'Would he see someone in Sydney if I set up an appointment? I know it's a long trip but surely it would be worth it to get him the help he needs.'

'He won't go back to the city, not after spending three months in hospital. He won't even go as far as Bourke.'

'Does he have any friends who could spend time

with him?' she asked. 'It might help lift his mood to be more active socially.'

The look he threw her was derisive. 'My father is not the tea-party type.'

'What about Margie Green?'

His brows came together. 'What about her?'

'She's a close friend, isn't she? Or she was in the old days before your parents got together.'

His expression was guarded now; the drawbridge had come up again. 'You seem to have gained a lot of inside information for the short time you've been in town.'

Izzy compressed her lips. 'I can't help it if people tell me stuff. I can assure you I don't go looking for it.'

He curled his lip in a mocking manner. 'I bet you don't.'

She picked up her doctor's bag from the floor with brisk efficiency. 'I think it's time I left. I've clearly outstayed my welcome.'

Izzy had marched to the front door before he caught up with her. 'Dr Courtney.' It was a command, not a request or even an apology. She drew in a tight breath and turned to face him. His expression still had that reserved unreadable quality to it but something about his eyes made her think he was not so much angry at her as at the situation he found himself in.

'Yes?'

He held her gaze for a long moment without speaking. It was as if he was searching through a filing drawer in his brain for the right words.

'*Yes?*' Izzy prompted.

'Don't give up on him.' He did that hair-scrape thing again. 'He needs time.'

'Will four weeks be long enough, do you think?' she asked.

He gave her another measured look before he opened the screen door for her. 'Let's hope so.'

'So, what did you call your new boyfriend I sent you?' Hannah asked when she video-messaged Izzy a couple of nights later.

Izzy looked at the blow-up male doll she had propped up in one of the armchairs in the sitting room. 'I've called him Max. He's surprisingly good company for a man. He doesn't hog the remote control and he doesn't eat all the chocolate biscuits.'

Hannah giggled. 'Have you slept with him?'

Izzy rolled her eyes. 'Ha-ha. I'm enjoying having the bed to myself, thank you very much.'

'So, no hot guys out in the bush?'

She hoped the webcam wasn't picking up the colour of her warm cheeks. She hadn't told Hannah about her case of mistaken identity with Zach Fletcher. She wasn't sure why. Normally she told Hannah everything that was going on in her life...well, maybe not *everything*. She had never been the type of girl to tell all about dates and boyfriends. There were some things she liked to keep private. 'I'm supposed to be using this time to sort myself out in the love department. I don't want to complicate my recovery by diving head first into another relationship.'

'You weren't in love with Richard, Izzy. You know you weren't. You were just doing what your parents expected of you. He filled the hole in your life after Jamie died. I'm glad you saw sense in time. Don't get me wrong—I really like Richard but he's not the one for you.'

Izzy knew what Hannah said was true. She had let things drift along for too long, raising everyone's hopes and expectations in the process. Her parents were still a little touchy on the subject of her split with Richard, whom they saw as the ideal son-in-law. The stand-in son for the one they had lost after a long and agonising battle with sarcoma.

Her decision to come out to the Australian Outback on a working holiday had been part of her strategy to take more control over her life. It was a way to remind her family that she was serious about her career. They still thought she was just dabbling at medicine until it was time to settle down and have a couple of children to carry on the long line of Courtney blood now that her older brother Jamie wasn't around to do it.

But she loved being a doctor. She loved it that she could help people in such a powerful way. Not just healing illnesses but changing lives, even saving them on occasion.

Like Jamie might have been saved if he had been diagnosed earlier...

Thinking about her brother made her heart feel like it had been stabbed. It actually seemed to jerk in her chest every time his name was mentioned, as if it were trying to escape the lunge of the sword of memory.

'Maybe you'll meet some rich cattleman out there and fall madly in love and never come home again, other than for visits,' Hannah said.

'I don't think that's likely.' Izzy couldn't imagine leaving England permanently. Her roots went down too deep. She even loved the capricious weather.

No, this trip out here was timely but not permanent.

Besides, with Jamie gone she was her parents' only child and heir. Not going home to claim her birthright would be unthinkable. She just needed a few months to let them get used to the idea of her living her own life and following her own dreams, instead of living vicariously through theirs.

Izzy's phone buzzed where it was plugged into the charger on the kitchen bench. 'Got to go, Han. I think that's a local call coming through. I'll call you in a day or two. Bye.' She picked up her phone. 'Isabella Courtney.'

'Zach Fletcher here.' Even the way he said his name was sharp and to the point.

'Good evening, Sergeant,' Izzy said, just as crisply. 'What can I do for you?'

'I just got a call about an accident out by the Honeywells' place. It doesn't sound serious but I thought you should come out with me to check on the driver. The volunteer ambos are on their way. I can be at your place in two minutes. It will save you having to find your way out there in the dark.'

'Fine. I'll wait at the front for you.'

Izzy had her doctor's bag at the ready when Zach pulled up outside her cottage. She got into the car and clipped on her seat belt, far more conscious than she wanted to be of him sitting behind the wheel with one of those unreadable expressions on his face.

Would it hurt him to crack a smile?

Say a polite hello?

Make a comment on the weather?

'Do you know who's had the accident?' she asked.

'Damien Redbank.' He gunned the engine once he

turned onto the highway and Izzy's spine slammed back against the seat. 'His father Charles is a big property owner out here. Loads of money, short on common sense, if you get my drift.'

Izzy sent him a glance. 'The son or the father?'

The top edge of his mouth curled upwards but it wasn't anywhere near a smile. 'The kid's all right. Just needs to grow up.'

'How old is he?'

'Eighteen and a train wreck waiting to happen.'

'What about his mother?'

'His parents are divorced. Vanessa Redbank remarried a few years ago.' He waited a beat before adding, 'She has a new family now.'

Izzy glanced at him again. His mouth had tightened into its default position of grim. 'Does Damien see his mother?'

'Occasionally.'

Occasionally probably wasn't good enough, Izzy thought. 'Where does she live?'

'Melbourne.'

'At least it's not the other side of the world.' She bit her lip and wished she hadn't spoken her thoughts out loud. 'I'm sorry...I hope I didn't offend you.'

He gave her a quick glance. 'Offend me how?'

Izzy tried to read his look but the mask was firmly back in place. 'It must have been really tough on you when your mother left. England is a long way away from here. It feels like *everywhere* is a long way away from here. It would've seemed even longer to a young child.'

'I wasn't a young child. I was ten.' His voice was stripped bare of emotion; as if he was reading from a script and not speaking from personal experience. 'Plenty old enough to take care of myself.'

Izzy could imagine him watching as his mother had driven away from the property for the last time. His face blank, his spine and shoulders stoically braced, while no doubt inside him a tsunami of emotion had been roiling. Had his father comforted him or had he been too consumed by his own devastation over the breakdown of his marriage? No wonder Zach had an aura of unreachability about him. It was a circle of deep loneliness that kept him apart from others. He didn't want to need people so he kept well back from them.

Unlike her, who felt totally crushed if everyone didn't take an instant shine to her. Doing and saying the right thing—*people-pleasing*—had been the script she had been handed from the cradle. It was only now that she had stepped off the stage, so to speak, that she could see how terribly lonely and isolated she had felt.

Still felt...

When had she not felt lonely? Being sent to boarding school hadn't helped. She had wanted to go to a day school close to home but her protests had been ignored. All Courtneys went to boarding school. It was a tradition that went back generations. It was what the aristocracy did. But Izzy had been too bookish and too shy to be the most popular girl. Not athletic enough to be chosen first, let alone be appointed the captain of any of the sporting teams. Too keen to please her teachers, which hadn't won her any friends. Too frightened to do the wrong thing in case she was made a spectacle of in front of the whole school. Until she'd met Hannah a couple of years later, her life had been terrifyingly, achingly lonely.

* * *

'When I was ten I still couldn't go to sleep unless all of my Barbie dolls were lined up in bed with me in exactly the right order.' *Why are you telling him this stuff?* 'I've still got them. Not with me, of course.'

Zach's gaze touched hers briefly. It was the first time she had seen a hint of a smile dare to come anywhere near the vicinity of his mouth. But just as soon as it appeared it vanished. He turned his attention back to the grey ribbon of road in front of them where in the distance Izzy could see the shape of a car wedged at a steep angle against the bank running alongside the road. Another car had pulled up alongside, presumably the person who had called for help.

'Damien's father's not going to be too happy about this,' Zach said. 'He's only had that car a couple of weeks.'

'But surely he'll be more concerned about his son?' Izzy said. 'Cars can be replaced. People can't.'

The line of his mouth tilted in a cynical manner as he killed the engine. 'Try telling Damien's mother that.'

CHAPTER FOUR

WHEN IZZY GOT to the car the young driver was sitting on the roadside, holding his right arm against his chest. 'Damien? Hi, I'm Isabella Courtney, the new locum doctor in town. I'm going to check you over. Is that OK?'

Damien gave her a belligerent look. 'I'm fine. I don't need a doctor. And before you ask—' he sent Zach a glance '—no, I wasn't drinking.'

'I still have to do a breathalyser on you, mate,' Zach said. 'It's regulation when there's been an accident.'

'A stupid wombat was in the middle of the road,' Damien said. 'I had to swerve to miss it.'

'That arm looks pretty uncomfortable,' Izzy said. 'How about I take a look at it and if it's not too bad we can send you home.'

He rolled his eyes in that universal teenage *this sucks* manner, but he co-operated while she examined him. He had some minor abrasions on his forehead and face but the airbag had prevented any major injury. His humerus, however, was angled and swollen, indicative of a broken arm. Izzy took his pulse and found it was very weak and the forearm looked dusky due to the artery being kinked at the fracture site.

'I'm going to have to straighten that arm to restore blood flow,' she said. 'I'll give you something to take the edge off it but it still might hurt a bit.' She took out a Penthrane inhalant, which would deliver rapid analgesia. 'Take a few deep breaths on this…yes, that's right. Good job.'

While Damien was taking deep breaths on the inhalant Izzy put traction on the arm and aligned it. He gave a yowl during the process but the pulse had come back into the wrist and the hand and forearm had pinked up.

'Sorry about that,' she said. 'You did really well. I'm going to put a splint on your arm so we can get you to hospital. You're going to need an orthopaedic surgeon to have a look at that fracture.'

Damien muttered a swear word under his breath. 'My dad is going to kill me.'

'I've just called him,' Zach said. 'He's on his way. The ambos are five minutes away,' he said to Izzy.

'Good,' Izzy said, as she unpacked the inflatable splint. The boy was shivering with shock by now so she gave him an injection of morphine. She was about to ask Zach to pass her the blanket out of the kit when he handed it to her. She gave him a smile. 'Mind-reader.'

He gave a shrug. 'Been at a lot of accidents.'

Izzy hated to think of how terrible some of them might have been. Cops and ambulance personnel were always at the centre of drama and tragedy. The toll it took on them was well documented. But out in the bush, where the officers often personally knew the victims, it was particularly harrowing.

The volunteer ambulance officers were two of the people Izzy had met the other night at the pub, Ken Gordon and Roger Parker. After briefing them on the boy's condition, she supervised them as they loaded Damien onto a stretcher, supporting his arm. And then, once he was loaded, she put in an IV and set some fluids running. The Royal Flying Doctor Service would take over once the ambulance had delivered the boy to the meeting point about eighty kilometres away.

Not long after the ambulance had left, a four-wheel-drive farm vehicle pulled up. A middle-aged man got out from behind the wheel and came over to where Zach was sorting out the towing of the damaged vehicle with the local farmer who had called in the accident.

'Is it a write-off?' Charles Redbank asked.

Izzy paused in the process of stripping off her sterile gloves. Although Zach had called Charles and told him Damien was OK, she still found it strange that he would want to check on the car before he saw his son. What sort of father was he? Was a car really more important to him than his own flesh and blood?

Zach put his pen back in his top pocket as he faced Charles. His mouth looked particularly grim. 'No.'

'Bloody fool,' Charles muttered. 'Was he drinking?'

'No.'

'He's not seriously hurt.' Izzy stepped forward. 'He has a broken arm that will need to be seen by an orthopaedic surgeon. I've arranged for him to be flown to Bourke. If you hurry you can catch up with the ambulance. It's only just left. You probably passed it on the road.'

'I came in on the side road from Turner's Creek,' Charles said. 'And you can think again if you think I'm going to chase after him just because he's got a broken arm. He can deal with it. He's an adult, or he's supposed to be.'

Yes, and he's had a great role model, Izzy thought. 'Damien will need a few things if he stays in hospital for a day or two. A change of clothes, a toothbrush, toiletries—that sort of thing.'

Charles gave her the once-over. 'Are you the new doctor?'

'Yes. Isabella Courtney.'

His eyes ran over her again, lingering a little too long on her breasts. 'Bit young to be a doctor, aren't you?'

Izzy had faced similar comments for most of her medical career. She did her best to not let it get to her. Just because she had a youthful appearance, it didn't mean she wasn't good at her job. 'I can assure you I am quite old enough and have all the necessary qualifications.'

'Your left brake light isn't working,' Zach said to Charles.

Charles rocked back on his heels, his gaze running between Izzy and Zach like a ferret's. 'So that's the way it is, is it? Well, well, well. You're a fast worker. She's only been in town, what, a couple of days?'

Zach's jaw looked like it had been set in place by an invisible clamp. 'I told you three weeks ago to get it fixed.'

Charles's smile was goading. 'She's a bit too upmarket for you, Fletch. And what would your old man say if you brought a posh Pommy girl home, eh? That'd go down a treat, wouldn't it?'

Izzy marvelled at Zach's self-control for even *she* felt like punching Charles Redbank. Zach looked down from his considerable height advantage at the farmer, his strong gaze unwavering. 'I'll give you twenty-four hours to get that light seen to. Ian Cooke is going to tow the car into Joe's workshop. He's gone back to town for the truck now. I'm heading to Bourke for a court appearance tomorrow. If you pack a few things for Damien, I'll swing by and pick them up before I leave in the morning.'

'Wouldn't want to put you to any trouble,' Charles said, with a deliberate absence of sincerity.

'It's no trouble,' Zach said. 'Damien's a good kid. He just needs a little direction.'

Charles's lip curled. 'What? And you think you're the one to give it to him?'

'That's your job,' Zach said, and turned away to leave. 'Coming, Dr Courtney?'

Izzy waited until they were in the car before she said, 'Is there a special section in the police training manual on how to handle jerks?'

He gave her a look as he started the engine. 'He's a prize one, isn't he?'

'You handled that situation so well. I was impressed.' She pulled down her seat belt and clicked it into place. 'Quite frankly, I wanted to punch him.'

'Two wrongs never make a right.'

Izzy studied him for a beat or two. 'Are you really going to Bourke for a court appearance tomorrow?'

He turned the car for town before he answered. 'I have the day off. It'll be an outing for my father if I can convince him to come. Take his mind off his own troubles for a change.'

'He's very lucky to have you.'

'He's a good dad. He's always tried to do his best, even under difficult circumstances.'

The township appeared in the distance, the sprinkling of lights glittering in the warm night air.

'You did a good job out there tonight.' Zach broke the silence that had fallen between them.

Izzy glanced at him again. 'You were expecting me not to, weren't you?'

'Have you worked in a remote region before?'

'I did a short stint in South Africa last year.'

His brows moved upwards. 'So why Outback Australia this year?'

'I've always wanted to come out here,' Izzy said. 'A lot of my friends had come out and told me how amazing it is. I spent a few days in Sydney on my way here. I'm looking forward to seeing a bit more after I finish my six months of locums. Melbourne, Adelaide, Perth, maybe a quick trip up to Broome and the Kimberleys.'

Another silence fell.

Izzy felt as if he was waiting for her to tell him her real reason for coming out here. It was what cops did. They waited. They listened. They observed. She had seen him looking at her ring hand while she'd been strapping up Damien. He'd been a cop too long to miss that sort of detail. 'I also wanted to get away from home for a while. My parents weren't too happy about me breaking off my engagement a couple of months ago.'

'How long were you engaged?'

'Four years.'

'Some people don't stay married that long.'

'True.' She waited a moment before saying, 'Margie told me you'd gone through a break-up a while back.'

'Yeah, well, I can't scratch my nose in this town without everyone hearing about it.' His tone was edgy, annoyed.

Izzy pushed on regardless. 'Were you together long?'

He threw her a hard glance. 'Why are you asking

me? Surely the locals have already given you all the gory details?'

'I'd like to hear it from you.'

He drove for another two kilometres or so before he spoke. 'We'd been seeing each other a year or so. We had only been engaged for a couple of months when my father had his accident.'

'So you came back home.'

'Yeah.'

'She didn't want to pull up stumps and come with you?'

'Nope.'

'I'm sorry.'

'Don't be. I'm not.' He pulled up in front of her cottage and swivelled in his seat to look at her. 'Was your fiancé a doctor?'

'A banker.' She put her hand on the door. 'Um, I should go in. It's getting late.'

'I'll walk you to the door.'

'That's not necessary...' It was too late. He was already out of the car and coming round to her side.

Izzy stepped out of the car but she misjudged the kerb and stumbled forward. Two iron-strong hands shot out and prevented her from falling. She felt every one of his fingers around her upper arms. That wasn't all she felt. Electric heat coursed through her from the top of her head to the balls of her feet. She could smell the scent of his skin, the sweat and dust and healthy male smell that was like a tantalising potion to her overly sanitised city nostrils. Her heart gave a skittish jump as she saw the way his grey-blue gaze tracked to her mouth. The pepper of his stubble was rough along his jaw, the vigorous regrowth a heady reminder of the potent hormones that marked him as a full-blooded man.

'You OK?' His fingers loosened a mere fraction as his eyes came back to hers.

'I—I'm fine...' She felt a blush run up over her skin, the heat coming from the secret core of her body. 'I'm not normally so clumsy.'

He released her and took a step backwards, his expression as unfathomable as ever. 'The ground is pretty rough out here. You need to take extra care until you find your feet.'

'I'll be careful.' Izzy pushed a strand of hair back off her face. 'Um, would you like to come in for a coffee?' *Oh. My. God. You just asked him in for coffee! What are you doing? Are you nuts?*

His brows twitched together. 'Coffee?'

'Don't all cops drink coffee? I have tea if you'd prefer. No doughnuts, I'm afraid. I guess it's kind of a cliché, you know, cops and doughnuts. I bet you don't even eat them.' *Stop talking!*

'Thanks, but no.'

No?

No?

It was hard not to feel slighted. Was she such hideous company that a simple coffee was out of the question? 'Fine.' Izzy forced a smile. 'Some other time, then.' She lifted a hand in a fingertip wave. 'Thanks for the lift. See you around.' She turned and walked quickly and purposefully to the cottage knowing he probably wouldn't drive away until she was safely inside.

'Dr Courtney.'

Izzy turned to see him holding her doctor's bag, which she had left on the back seat of his car. Her cheeks flared all over again. What was it about him that made her brain turn to scrambled mush? 'Oh… right. Might need that.'

He brought her bag to her on the doorstep, his fingers brushing against hers as he handed it over. The shock of his touch thrilled her senses all over again and her heart gave another skip-hop-skip inside her chest. The flecks of blue in his eyes seemed even darker than ever, his pupils black, bottomless inkwells.

'Thanks.' Her voice came out like a mouse squeak.

'You're welcome.'

The crackle of the police radio in the car sounded excessively loud. Jarring.

He gave her one of his curt nods and stepped down off the veranda, walking the short distance to his car, getting behind the wheel and driving off, all within the space of a few seconds.

Izzy slowly released her breath as she watched his taillights disappear into the distance.

Stop that thought.

You did not come all this way to make your life even more complicated.

Zach found his father sitting out on the southern side of the veranda when he got back to the homestead. He let out the tight breath he felt like he'd been holding all day and let his shoulders go down with it. 'Fancy a run out to Bourke tomorrow?'

'What for?'

'Damien Redbank had an accident this evening. He's fine, apart from a broken arm. He'll be in hospital a couple of days. I thought he could do with some company.'

'What's wrong with his father?'

'Good question.' Zach took off his police hat and raked his hands through his sweat-sticky hair.

Doug gave him a probing look. 'You OK?'

Zach tossed his hat onto the nearest cane chair. 'I've never felt more like punching someone's lights out.'

'Understandable. Charles has been pressing your buttons for a while now.'

'He's incompetent as a father,' Zach said. 'He's got no idea how to be a role model for that kid. No wonder the boy is running amok. He's crying out for someone to take notice of him. To show they care about him.'

'The boy hasn't been the same since his mother remarried.'

Zach grunted. 'Yeah, I know.'

The crickets chirruped in the garden below the veranda.

'What time are you thinking of heading out of town?' Doug asked.

'Sixish.'

A stone curlew let out its mournful cry and Popeye lifted his little black head off the faded cushion on the seat beside Zach's father's chair, but seeing Zach's stay signal quickly settled back down again with a little doggy sigh and closed his eyes.

'How'd the new doctor handle things?' Doug asked.

'Better than I thought she would, but it's still early days.'

His father slanted him a glance. 'Watch your step, son.'

'I'm good.'

'Yeah, that's we all say. Next thing you know she'll have your heart in a vice.'

'Not going to happen.' Zach opened and closed his

fingers where the tingling of Izzy's touch had lingered far too long. It had taken a truckload of self-control to decline her offer of coffee. Even if she had just been being polite in asking him in, he hadn't wanted to risk stepping over the boundaries.

His body had other ideas, of course. But he was going to have to tame its urges if he was to get through this next month without giving in to temptation. A fling with her would certainly break the dogged routine he'd slipped into but how would he feel when she packed her bags and drove out of town?

He had to concentrate on his father's health right now.

That was the priority.

Distractions—even ones as delightfully refreshing and dazzling as Izzy Courtney—would have to wait.

CHAPTER FIVE

IZZY REALISED ON her fourth patient the following morning that a rumour had been circulated about her and Zach Fletcher. Ida Jensen, a seventy-five-year-old farmer's wife, had come in to have her blood pressure medication renewed, but before Izzy could put the cuff on her arm to check her current reading, the older woman launched into a tirade.

'In my day a girl wouldn't dream of sleeping with a man before she was married, especially with a man she's only just met.' She pursed her lips in a disapproving manner. 'I don't know what the world's coming to, really I don't. Everyone having casual flings as if love and commitment mean nothing. It's shameful, that's what it is.'

'I guess not everyone shares the same values these days,' Izzy said, hoping to prevent an extended moral lecture.

'I blame the Pill. Girls don't have to worry about falling pregnant so they just do what they want with whoever they want. That boy needs a wife, not a mistress.'

'That...er, boy?'

'Zach Fletcher,' Ida said. 'Don't bother trying to deny it. Everyone knows you've got your eye on him, and him not even over the last one. Mind you, they do say you should get back on the horse, don't they? Never did like that saying. It's a bit coarse, if you ask me. But I think he needs more time. What if his ex changes her mind and comes out here to see you're involved with him?'

'I beg your pardon?'

Ida shifted in her chair like a broody hen settling on a clutch of eggs. 'Not that anyone could really blame you, of course. No one's saying he isn't good looking. Got a nice gentle nature too, when you get to know him.'

Izzy frowned. 'I'm sorry but I'm not sure where you got the idea that I'm involved with Sergeant Fletcher.'

'Don't bother denying it,' Ida said. 'I heard it from a very reliable source. Everyone's talking about it.'

'Then they can stop talking about it because it's not true!' Izzy was fast becoming agitated. 'Have you asked Sergeant Fletcher about this? I suggest you do so you can hear it from him as well that nothing is going on. This is nothing more than scurrilous gossip.' *And I have a feeling I know who started it.*

'Are you sure it's not true?' Ida looked a little uncomfortable.

'I think I would know who I was or wasn't sleeping with, don't you?' Izzy picked up the blood-pressure cuff. 'Now, let's change the subject, otherwise my blood pressure is going to need medication.'

'What? Don't you fancy him?' Ida asked after a moment.

Izzy undid the cuff from the older woman's arm and wrote the figure in her notes. 'I see here you're taking anti-inflammatories for your arthritis. Any trouble with your stomach on that dosage?'

'Not if I take them with food.'

'Is there anything else I can help you with?'

The older woman folded her lips together. 'I hope I haven't upset you.'

'Not at all,' Izzy lied.

'It's just we all love Zach so much. We want him to be happy.'

'I'm sure he appreciates your concern but he's a big boy and can surely take care of himself.'

'That's half the trouble...' Ida let out a heartfelt sigh. 'He's been taking care of himself for too long.'

Izzy stood up to signal the end of the consultation. 'Make another appointment to see me in a week. I'd like to keep an eye on your blood pressure. It was slightly elevated.'

Just like mine.

'Nice work, Fletch,' Jim Collis said, when Zach came in the next morning for the paper.

Zach didn't care for the ear-to-ear grin the store-keeper was wearing. 'What?'

Jim had hooked his thumbs in his belt and tilted backwards on his heels behind the counter. 'Getting it on with the new doctor. Talk about a fast mover. You want me to stock up on condoms?'

Zach kept his expression closed as he picked up a stock magazine his father enjoyed, as well as the paper. He put them both on the counter and took out his wallet. 'You should check your sources before you start spreading rumours like that.'

'You telling me it's not true?'

'Even if it was true, I wouldn't be standing here discussing it.'

'Charles Redbank seemed pretty convinced you two

were getting it on,' Jim said. 'Not that anyone would blame you for making a move on her. Be a good way to get that Naomi chick out of your system once and for all.'

Zach ground his molars together. It got under his skin that the whole town saw him as some sort of broken-hearted dude let down by his fiancée. He was over Naomi. It had been a convenient relationship that had worked well for both of them until he'd made the decision to come back to Jerringa Ridge to help his father. Yes, he was a little pissed off she hadn't wanted to come with him but that was her loss. In time he would find someone to fill her place, but he needed to get his father sorted out first.

'Anyway, way I see it,' Jim went on, 'if you don't hit on Izzy Courtney then you can bet your bottom dollar some other fella soon will.' He cleared his throat as the screen door opened. 'Hi, Dr Courtney, I got that honey and cinnamon yogurt you wanted.'

Zach hitched his hip as he put his wallet in his back pocket before turning to look at her. 'G'day.'

'Hello…' The blush on her cheeks was like the petals of a pink rose. She looked young and fresh, like a model from a fashion magazine. Her simple flowered cotton dress was cinched in at her tiny waist, her legs were bare and her feet in ballet flats. She had a string of pearls around her neck that were a perfect foil for her milk-pure skin. And even with all the other competing smells of the general store he could still pick up her light gardenia scent. It occurred to him to wonder why anyone would wear pearls in the Outback but it was something his mother had done and he knew from experience there was no explaining it.

'So, I'll get those condoms in for you, will I, Fletch?' Jim said with a cheeky grin. 'Extra-large, wasn't it?'

The blush on Izzy Courtney's cheeks intensified. Her eyes slipped out of reach of his and her teeth snagged at her full lower lip. 'Maybe I'll come back later...' She turned and went back out the screen door so quickly it banged loudly on its hinges.

Zach scooped up the paper and the magazine, giving Jim a look that would have cut through steel. 'You're a freaking jerk, you know that?'

Izzy turned at the sound of firm footsteps to find Zach coming towards her. That fluttery sensation she always got when she saw him tickled the floor of her stomach like an ostrich feather held by someone with a tremor. His mouth was tightly set, his expression formidable this time rather than masked. Her earlier blush still hadn't completely died down but as soon as his eyes met hers she felt it heat up another few degrees.

'We need to talk.' He spoke through lips so tight they barely moved.

'We do?' She saw his dark frown and continued, 'Yes, of course we do. Look, it's fine. It's just a rumour. It'll go away when they realise there's no truth in it.'

'I'm sorry but this is what happens in small country towns.'

'I realise that,' Izzy said. 'I've already had a couple of stern lectures from some of the more conservative elders in the community. It seems that out here it's still a sin for a woman to have sex before marriage. Funny, but they didn't mention it being a sin for men. That really annoys me. Why should you men have all the fun?'

His gaze briefly touched her mouth before glancing away to look at something in the distance, his eyes squinting against the brutal sunlight. 'Not all of us are having as much fun as you think.'

Izzy moistened her suddenly dry lips. 'How is your father? Did he go with you to Bourke?'

'Yes.'

'And how was Damien?'

'Feeling a bit sorry for himself.'

'Did his father end up going to see him?' Izzy brushed a wisp of hair away from her face.

He made a sound that sounded somewhere between a grunt and a laugh. 'No.'

'I guess he was too busy spreading rumours back here.'

His brooding frown was a deep V between his brows. 'I should've punched him when I had the chance.'

She studied Zach for a moment. Even without his uniform he still maintained that aura of command and control. She wondered what it would take to get under his skin enough to make him break out of that thick veneer of reserve. There was a quiet intensity about him, as if inside he was bottling up emotions he didn't want anyone to see. 'You don't seem the type of guy to throw the first punch.'

'Yeah, well, I don't get paid to pick fights.' He drew in a breath and released it in a measured way as if he was rebalancing himself. 'I'd better let you get to work. Have a good one.'

Izzy watched as he strode back to where his car was parked outside the general store. She too let out a long breath, but any hope of rebalancing herself was as likely as a person on crutches trying to ice-skate.

Not going to happen.

* * *

Almost a week went past before Izzy saw Zach again other than from a distance. Although they worked within a half a block of each other, he was on different shifts and she spent most days inside the clinic, other than a couple of house calls she had made out of town. But each time she stepped outside the clinic or her cottage or drove out along any of the roads she mentally prepared herself for running into him.

She had seen him coming out of the general store one evening as she'd been leaving work, but he'd been on the phone and had seemed preoccupied, and hadn't noticed her at all. For some reason that rankled. It didn't seem fair that she was suffering heart skips and stomach flips at the mere mention of his name and yet he didn't even sense her looking at him. Neither did he even glance at the clinic just in case she was coming out.

Izzy still had to field the occasional comment from a patient but she decided that was the price of being part of a small community. You couldn't sneeze in a town the size of Jerringa Ridge without everyone saying you had flu.

But on Saturday night, just as she was thinking about going to bed, she got a call from Jim Collis, who was down at the pub. 'Been a bit of trouble down here, Doc,' he said. 'Thought you might want to look in on Zach if you've got a minute. I reckon he might need a couple of stitches.'

'What happened?'

'Couple of the young fellas had too much to drink and got a bit lively. Zach's down at the station, waiting for the parents to show up. I told him to call you but he said it's just a bruise. Don't look like a bruise to me. He's lucky he didn't lose an eye, if you ask me.'

'I'll head down straight away.'

Izzy turned up the station just as a middle-aged couple came out with their son. The smell of alcohol was sour in the air as they walked past to bundle him into the car. The mother looked like she had been crying and the father looked angry enough to throw something. The son looked subdued but it was hard to tell if that was the excess alcohol taking effect or whether he'd faced charges.

When she went inside the building Zach was sitting behind the desk with a folded handkerchief held up to his left eye as he wrote some notes down on a sheet of paper. He glanced up and frowned at her. 'Who called you?'

'Jim Collis.'

He let out a muffled expletive. 'He had no right to do that.' He pushed back from the desk and stood up. 'It's nothing. Just a scratch.'

'Why don't you let me be the judge of that?' She held up her doctor's bag. 'I've come prepared.'

He let out a long breath as if he couldn't be bothered arguing and led the way out to the small kitchen area out the back. 'Make it snappy. I need to get home.'

Izzy pushed one of the two chairs towards him. 'Sit.'

'Can't you do it standing up?'

'I'm not used to doing it standing up…' A hot blush stormed into her cheeks when she saw the one-eyed glinting look he gave her. 'I mean…you're way too tall for me to reach you.' *God, that sounded almost worse!*

He sat in the chair with his long legs almost cutting

the room in half. She had nowhere to stand other than between them to get close enough to inspect his eye. She was acutely aware of the erotic undertones as his muscled legs bracketed her body. They weren't touching her at all but she felt the warmth of his thighs like the bars of a radiator. Her mind went crazy with images of him holding her between those powerful thighs, his body pumping into hers, those muscled arms pinning her against the bed, a wall, or some other surface. Scorching heat flowed through her veins even as she slammed the brakes on her wickedly wanton thoughts.

Doctor face. Doctor face. Mentally chanting it was the only way she could get herself back on track. She gently took the wadded handkerchief off his eye to find it bruised and swollen with a split in the skin above his eyebrow that was still oozing blood. 'You won't need stitches but you'll have a nice shiner by morning.'

He grunted. 'Told you it was nothing.'

Izzy's leg bumped against his as she reached for some antiseptic in her bag. It was like being touched with a laser—the tingles went right to her core. She schooled her features as she turned back to tend to his cut. *Cool and clinical. Cool and clinical.* She could do that. She always did that...well; she did when it was anyone other than Zach Fletcher.

She could hear his breathing; it was slow and even, unlike hers, which was shallow and picking up pace as every second passed.

His scent teased her nostrils, making her think of sun-warmed lemons. He had a decent crop of prickly stubble on his jaw. She felt it catch on the sensitive skin on the underside of her wrist as she dabbed at his wound. 'I'm sorry if this hurts. I'm just cleaning the area before I put on a Steri-strip to hold the edges of the wound together.'

'Can't feel a thing.'

She carefully positioned the Steri-strip over the wound. 'There. Now, all we need is some ice for that eye. Do you have any in the fridge?'

'I'll put some on at home.'

He got to his feet at the same time as she reached to dab at a smear of blood on his cheek. He put his hands on her each of her forearms, presumably to stop her fussing over him, but somehow his fingers slid down to her wrists, wrapping around them like a pair of handcuffs.

Izzy felt her breath screech to a halt as his hooded gaze went to her mouth. The tip of her tongue came out and moistened the sudden dryness of her lips. He was so close she could feel the fronts of his muscle-packed thighs against hers.

He looked at her mouth and her belly did a little somersault as she saw the way his eyes zeroed in on it, as if he was memorising its contours. 'This is a really dumb idea.'

'It is? I mean, yes, *of course* it is,' Izzy said a little breathlessly. 'An absolutely crazy thing to do. What were we thinking? Hey, is that a smile? I didn't think you knew how to.'

'I'm a little out of practice.' He brought her even closer, his warm vanilla- and milk-scented breath skating over the surface of her lips. 'Isn't there some rule about doctors getting involved with their patients?'

'I'm not really your doctor. Not officially. I mean I treated you, but *I* came to see you. You didn't come to see me. It's not the same as if you'd made an appointment and paid me to see you. I just saw you as a one-off. A favour, if you like. It's not even going on the record. All I did was put a Steri-strip on your head. You could have done it yourself.' She took a much-needed breath. 'Um…you're not really going to kiss me, are you?'

His grey-blue eyes smouldered. 'What do you think?'

Izzy couldn't think, or at least not once his mouth came down and covered hers. His mouth was firm and warm and tasted of salt and something unexpectedly sinful. His tongue flickered against the seam of her mouth, a teasing come-play-with-me-if-you-dare gesture that made her insides turn to liquid. She opened her mouth and he entered it with a sexy glide of his tongue that made the hairs on her scalp stand up on tiptoe, one by one. He found her tongue with devastating expertise, toying with it, cajoling it into a dance as old as time.

He put a hand on the small of her back and pressed her closer. The feel of his hot urgent male body against her called to everything that was female in her. She had always struggled with desire in the past. She could talk herself into it eventually, but it had never been an instantaneous reaction.

Now it was like a dam had burst. Desire flowed through her like a flash flood, making her flesh cry out for skin-on-skin contact. Her hands came up to link around his neck, her body pressing even closer against his. Her breasts tingled behind the lace of her bra; she had never been more aware of her body, how it felt, what it craved, how it responded.

He gave a low, deep sound of pleasure and deepened the kiss, his hands going to both of her hips and locking her against him. She felt the hardened ridge of him against her and a wave of want coursed through her so rampantly it took her breath away.

She started on his shirt, pulling it out of his trousers and snapping open the buttons so she could glide her hands over his muscled chest. She could feel his heart beneath her palm. Thud. Thud. Thud. She could feel where his heart had pumped his blood in preparation. It throbbed against her belly with a primal beat that reso- nated through her body like a deep echo, making her insides quiver and reverberate with longing.

He kept kissing her, deeply and passionately, as his hands ran up under her light cotton shirt. The feel of his broad, warm, work-roughened hands on her skin made her gasp out loud. Her blood felt like it was on fire as it raced through her veins at torpedo speed.

Her inner wild woman had been released. Uncaged. Unrestrained. And the wild man in him was more than up to the task of taming her. She felt it in the way he was kissing her.

This was a kiss that meant business.

This was a kiss that said sex was next.

His hands found her breasts, pushing aside the con- fines of her bra to cup her skin on skin. She shivered as his thumbs rolled each of her nipples in turn; all while his mouth continued its mind-blowing assault on her senses.

The sound of the door opening at the front had Izzy springing back from him as if someone had fired a gun. She assiduously avoided Zach's gaze as she tidied her clothes with fingers that refused to co-operate.

'You there, Fletch?' Jim Collis called out.

'Yeah. Won't be a tick.' Zach redid the buttons be- fore tucking in his shirt. Izzy envied his cool cop composure as he went out to talk to Jim. Her nerves were in shreds at almost being discovered making out like teenagers in the back room.

'Is the doc still with you?' Jim asked.

There was a moment of telling silence.

'Yes, I'm still here.' Izzy stepped out, carrying her doctor's bag and what she hoped passed for doctor-just-finished-a-consult composure. 'I'm just leaving.'

Jim's eyes twinkled knowingly. 'So you've got him all sorted?'

'Er, yes.' She pasted on a tight smile. 'No serious damage done.'

'I hope you weren't annoyed with me, Fletch, for sending her over to patch you up?' Jim said.

Zach still had his cop face on. 'Not at all. She was very…professional.'

'Did you charge Adam Foster with assault?'

'Not this time. I gave him a warning.'

'You're too soft,' Jim said. 'Don't you think so, Dr Courtney?'

Izzy blushed to the roots of her hair. 'Um, it's late. I have to get home.' She gripped the handle of her bag and swung for the door. 'Goodnight.'

CHAPTER SIX

'WHAT HAPPENED TO your eye?' Doug Fletcher asked the following morning.

'I got in the way of Adam Foster's elbow.' Zach switched on the kettle. The less he talked about last night the better. The less *he thought* about last night the better. He had barely been able to sleep for thinking about Izzy Courtney's hot little mouth clamped to his, not to mention her hot little hands winding around his neck and smoothing over his chest. Even taking into account his eighteen-month sex drought, he couldn't remember ever being so turned on before. He had always prided himself on his self-control. But as soon as his mouth had connected with hers something had short-circuited in his brain.

He gave himself a mental shake and took out a couple of cups from the shelf above the sink. 'You want tea or coffee?'

'What did the doctor say?'

He frowned as he faced his father. 'What makes you think I saw the doctor? It's just a little cut and a black eye, for pity's sake. I don't know what all the fuss is about.'

His father gave him a probing look. 'Is it true?'

'Is what true?'

'The rumour going around town that you're sleeping with her.'

'Where'd you hear that?'

'Bill Davidson dropped in last night while you were at work. Said his wife Jean saw the doctor a couple of days back. She said the doctor blushed every time your name was mentioned.'

'Oh, for God's sake.' Zach wrenched open the fridge door for the milk.

'Find yourself another woman, by all means, but make sure she's a country girl who'll stick around,' his father said.

'Dad, give it a break. I'm not going to lose my head or my heart to Dr Courtney. She's not my type.'

'Your mother wasn't my type either but that didn't stop me falling in love with her, and look how that ended up.'

Zach let out a long breath. 'You really need to let it go. Mum's never coming back. You have to accept it.'

'She hasn't even called, not once. Not even an email or a get-well card.'

'That's because you told her never to contact you again after she forgot my thirtieth birthday, remember?'

His father scowled. 'What sort of mother forgets her own son's birthday?'

A mother who has two other younger sons she loves more, Zach thought. 'What do you want for breakfast?'

'Nothing.'

'Come on. You have to have something.'

'I'm not hungry.'

'Are you in pain?' Zach asked.

His father glowered. 'Stop fussing.'

'You must be getting pretty low on painkillers. You want me to get Dr Courtney to write a prescription for you?'

'I'll manage.'

He threw his father an exasperated look. 'How'd you get to be so stubborn? No wonder Mum walked out on you.'

His father's eyes burned with bitterness. 'That may be why she walked out on me but why'd she leave you?'

It was a question Zach had asked himself a thousand times. And all these years later he still didn't have an answer other than the most obvious.

She hadn't loved him enough to stay.

'So how are you and Zach getting on?' Margie asked on Monday morning.

Izzy worked extra-hard to keep her blush at bay. 'Fine.'

'Jim told me you saw to Zach's eye on Saturday night.'

'Yes.' Izzy kept her voice businesslike and efficient. 'Do you have Mrs Patterson's file there? I have to check on something.'

Margie handed the file across the counter. 'The Shearers' Ball is on the last weekend of your locum. Did Peggy tell you about it? It's to raise money for the community centre. It's not a glamorous shindig, like you'd have in England or anything. Just a bit of a bush dance and a chance to let your hair down. Will I put you down as a yes?'

It sounded like a lot of fun. Would Zach be there? Her insides gave a funny little skip at the thought of those strong arms holding her close to him in a waltz or a barn dance. 'I'll have a think about it.'

'Oh, but you must come!' Margie insisted. 'You'll have heaps of fun. People drive in from all over the district to come to it. We have a raffle and door prizes. It's the social event of the year. Everyone will be so disappointed if you don't show up. It'll be our way of thanking you for stepping in while William Sawyer and his wife were on holiday. They come every year without fail.'

Izzy laughed in defeat. 'All right. Sign me up.'

'Fabulous.' Margie grinned. 'Now I can twist Zach's arm.'

Izzy left the clinic at lunchtime to pick up the sandwich she'd ordered at the corner store. Jim gave her a wink and a cheeky smile as she came in. 'How's the patient?'

She looked at him blankly, even though she knew exactly which patient he meant. 'Which patient?'

'You don't have to be coy with me, Izzy. I know what you two were up to out back the other night. About time Zach got himself back out there. I bet that ex-fiancée of his hasn't spent the last eighteen months pining his absence.'

She kept her features neutral. 'Is my salad sandwich ready?'

'Yep.' He handed it over the counter, his grin still in place. 'Do me a favour?' He passed over another sandwich-sized package in a brown paper bag. 'Drop that in to Zach on your way past.'

Izzy took the package with a forced smile. 'Will do.'

Zach looked up when the door opened. Izzy was standing there framed by the bright sunlight. She was wearing trousers and a cotton top today but she looked no less feminine. Her hair was in one of those up styles that somehow managed to look makeshift and elegant at the same time. There was a hint of gloss on her lips, making them look even more kissable. He wondered what flavour it was today. Strawberry? Or was it raspberry again?

'Jim sent me with your lunch.' She passed it over the counter, her cheeks going a light shade of pink. He'd never known a woman to blush so much. What was going on inside that pretty little head of hers? Was she thinking of that kiss? Had she spent the night feeling restless and edgy while her body had throbbed with unmet needs, like his had?

'Thanks.' He stood up and put the sandwich to one side. 'I was going to call you about my father.'

'Oh?' Her expression flickered with concern. 'Is he unwell?'

'He's running out of prescription painkillers.'

She chewed at her lip. 'I'd have to officially see him before I'd write a script. There can be contraindications with other medications and so on.'

'Of course. I'll see if I can get him to come to the clinic.'

She shifted her weight from foot to foot. 'I could always come out again to the homestead, if you think he'd allow it. I know what it's like to have something unexpected sprung on you. Maybe if you told him ahead of time that I was coming out, he would be more amenable to seeing me.'

'I'll see what I can do.'

The elephant in the room was stealing all the oxygen out of the air.

'What about coming out for dinner tomorrow?' Zach

could hardly believe he had spoken the words until he heard them drop into the ringing silence.

Her eyes widened a fraction. 'Dinner?'

'It won't be anything fancy. I'm not much of a chef but I can rub a couple of ingredients together.'

'What about your dad?'

'He has to eat.'

'I know, but will he agree to eat if I'm there?'

He shrugged, as if he didn't care either way. 'Let's give it a try, shall we?'

Her eyes went to the Steri-strip above his eyebrow. 'Would you like me to check that wound for you?'

Zach wanted her to check every inch of his body, preferably while both of them were naked. He had to blink away the erotic image that flashed through his brain at that thought—her limbs entangled with his, his body plunging into hers. 'It's fine.'

Her gaze narrowed as she peered at him over the bridge of the desk. 'It looks a little red around the edges.'

So do your cheeks, he thought. Her eyes were remarkably steady on his, but he had a feeling she was working hard at keeping them there. 'It's not infected. I'm keeping an eye on it.'

'Right...well, if you think it's not healing properly let me know.'

Zach couldn't figure if it was her in particular or the thought of having sex again that was making him so horny. He had tried his best to avoid thinking about sex for months. But now Izzy Courtney, with her toffee-brown eyes and soft, kissable mouth, was occupying his thoughts and he was in a constant start of arousal. He could feel it now, the pulse of his blood ticking through his veins. His heightened awareness of her sweet, fresh scent, the way his hands wanted to stroke down the length of her arms, to encircle her slim wrists, to tug her up against him so she could feel the weight and throb of his erection before his mouth closed over hers.

Her gaze flicked to his mouth, as if she had read his mind, the point of her tongue sneaking out to moisten her plump, soft lips. 'Um… What time do you want me to come?' Her cheeks went an even darker shade of red. 'Er…tonight. For dinner. To see your dad.'

'Seven or thereabouts?'

'Lovely.' She backed out of the reception area but somehow managed to bump her elbow against the door as she turned on her way out. She stepped out into the bright sunshine and walked briskly down the steps and out of sight.

Zach didn't sit down again until the fragrance of her had finally disappeared.

'What do you mean, you're going out?' Zach asked his father that evening.

His father gave him an offhand glance. 'I'm entitled to a social life, aren't I?'

'Of course.' Zach raked a distracted hand through his hair. 'But tonight of all nights? You haven't been out for months.'

'It's been a while since I caught up with Margie Green. She invited me for dinner.'

'She's been inviting you for dinner for years and you've always declined.'

'Then it's high time I said yes. You're always on about me not socialising enough. I enjoyed that run up to Bourke. It made me realise I need to have a change of scene now and again.'

Zach frowned. 'Isabella Courtney is going to think I've set this up. I asked her to come out to see you, not me.'

'She can think what she likes,' his father said. 'Anyway, I don't want to cramp your style.'

'But what about your painkillers?' Zach asked. 'You know what your rehab specialist said. You have to stay in front of the pain, not chase it.'

Doug chewed that over for a moment. 'I'll think about going to the clinic in a day or two.' A car horn tooted outside. 'That's Margie now.' He shuffled to the door on his frame. 'Don't wait up.'

Within a few minutes of his father leaving with Margie, Izzy arrived. Zach held open the door for her while Popeye danced around her like he had springs on his paws. 'My father's gone out. You probably passed him on the driveway.'

'Yes, Margie waved to me on the way past. I bet she's pleased he finally agreed to have dinner with her.' She picked Popeye up and cuddled him beneath her chin. 'Hello, sweetie pie.'

Zach was suddenly jealous of his dog, who was nestled against the gentle swell of Izzy's breasts. He gave himself a mental kick. He had to stop thinking of that kiss. It was becoming an obsession. 'Why's that?'

'I think she's been in love with him for years,' she said, and Popeye licked her face enthusiastically, as if in agreement.

'She's wasting her time,' Zach said. 'My father is still in love with my mother.'

She put the dog back down on the floor before she faced him. 'Do you really think so?'

He looked into her beautiful brown eyes, so warm

and soft, like melted caramel. The lashes like miniature fans. She seemed totally unaware of how beautiful she was. Unlike his ex, Naomi, who hadn't been able to walk past a mirror or a plate of glass without checking her reflection to check that her hair and make-up were perfect.

Another mental kick.

Harder this time.

'He's never looked at anyone else since.'

'Doesn't mean he still loves her. Some men have a lot of trouble with letting go of bitterness after a break-up.'

Zach coughed out a disparaging laugh. 'How long does he need? Isn't a couple of decades long enough?'

She gave a little lip-shrug. 'I guess some men are more stubborn than others.'

He wondered if she was having a little dig at his own stubbornness. He knew he should have found someone else by now. Most men would have done. It wasn't that he wasn't ready… He just hadn't met anyone who made him feel like…well, like Izzy did. Hot. Bothered. Hungry.

At this rate he was going to knock himself unconscious with all those mental kicks. 'What would you like to drink? I have white wine, red wine or beer…or something soft?'

'A small glass of white wine would be lovely.' She handed him a small container she was carrying. 'Um…I made these. I thought your father might enjoy them.'

He opened the plastic container to find home-baked chocolate-chip cookies inside. The smell of sugar and chocolate was like ambrosia. 'His favourite.' *And mine.* He met her gaze again. 'How'd you guess?'

She gave him a wry smile. 'I don't know too many men who would turn their nose up at home baking.'

'The way to a man's heart and all that.'

She looked taken aback. 'I wasn't trying to—'

'He'll love you for it. Eventually.'

After he'd put the cookies aside he handed her a glass of wine. 'Have you had the hard word put on you about the Shearers' Ball yet?'

'Margie twisted my arm yesterday to sign up. You?'

'I swear every year I'm not going to go and somehow someone always manages to convince me to show up if I'm in town. I try to keep a low profile. I'm seen as the fun police even when I'm not in uniform.'

'I've never been to a bush dance before. Is it very hard to learn the steps?'

'No, there's a caller. That's usually Bill Davidson. He's been doing it for years. His father did it before him. You'll soon get the hang of it.'

'I hope so…'

He couldn't stop looking at her mouth, how softly curved it was, how it had felt beneath the firm pressure of his. Desire was already pumping through his body. Just looking at her was enough to set him off. She was dressed in one of her simple dresses, black, sleeveless and just over the knee, with nothing but the flash of a small diamond pendant around her neck. There were diamond studs in her ears and her hair was in a high ponytail that swished from side to side when she walked. She had put on the merest touch of make-up: a neutral shade of eyeshadow with a fine line of kohl pencilled on her eyelids and beneath her eyes, emphasising the dark thickness of her lashes.

Zach cleared his throat. It was time to get the elephant on its way. 'Look, about the other night when I—'

'It's fine.' She gave him another little twisted smile. 'Really. It was just a kiss.'

'I wouldn't want you to get the wrong idea about me.' He pushed a hand through his hair. 'Contrary to what you might think, I'm not the sort of guy to feel up a woman as soon as he gets her alone.'

Her gaze slipped away from his. 'It was probably my fault.'

He frowned down at her. 'How was it *your* fault? I made the first move.'

'I kissed you back.' She bit her lower lip momentarily. 'Rather enthusiastically, if I recall.'

He *did* recall.

He could recall every thrilling moment of that kiss.

The trouble was he wanted to repeat it. But a relationship with Izzy would be distracting, to say the least. He had to concentrate on getting his dad as independent as he could before he spared a thought to what *he* wanted. He hadn't been that good at balancing the demands of a relationship and work in the past. It would be even worse now with his dad's needs front and centre. He couldn't spread himself any thinner than he was already doing.

His ex had always been on at him to give more of himself but he hadn't felt comfortable with that level of emotional intimacy. He had loved Naomi…or at least he thought he had. Sometimes he wondered if he'd just loved being part of a couple. That was a large part of the reason he'd agreed to her moving in with him. Having someone there to share the sofa with while he zoned out the harrowing demands of the day in front of the television or over a meal he hadn't had to cook.

He sounded like a chauvinist, but after living alone with his dad for all those years he'd snapped up Naomi's willingness to take over the kitchen. Asking her to marry him had been the logical next step. Her refusal to move to the country with him after his father's accident had been not so much devastating as disappointing. He was disappointed in himself. Why had he thought she would follow him wherever life took him? She had her own career. It was unfair of him to demand her to drop everything and come with him. And living in the dry, dusty Outback on a sheep property with a partially disabled and disgruntled father-in-law was a big ask.

Zach blinked himself out of the past. 'Do you want to eat outside? There's a nice breeze coming in from the south. Dad and I often eat out there when a southerly is due.'

'Lovely. Can I help bring anything out?'

He handed her a pair of salad servers and a bottle of dressing.

Her fingers brushed against his as she took the bottle from him and a lightning-fast sensation went straight to his groin. He felt the stirring of his blood; the movement of primal instinctive flesh that wanted something he had denied it for too long.

Her eyes met his, wide, doe-like, the pupils enlarged. Her tongue—*the tongue he had intimately stroked and sucked and teased*—darted out over her lips in a nervous sweeping action. He caught a whiff of her fragrance, wisteria this time instead of gardenias, but just as alluring.

But then the moment passed.

She seemed to mentally gather herself, and with another one of those short on-off smiles she turned in the direction of the veranda, her ponytail swinging behind her.

Zach looked down at Popeye, who was looking up at him with a quizzical expression in those black button eyes. 'Easy for you. You've had the chop. I have to suffer the hard way. No pun intended.'

CHAPTER SEVEN

Izzy put the salad servers and the dressing on the glass-topped white cane table then turned and looked at the view from the veranda. The paddocks stretched far into the distance where she could see a line of trees where the creek snaked in a sinuous curve along the boundary of the property. The air was warm with that hint of eucalyptus she was coming to love. It was such a distinctive smell, sharp and cleansing. The setting sun had painted the sky a dusky pink, signalling another fine day for tomorrow, and a flock of kookaburras sounded in the trees by the creek, their raucous call fracturing the still evening air like the laughter of a gang of madmen.

She turned when she heard the firm tread of Zach's footsteps on the floorboards of the veranda. Popeye was following faithfully, his bright little eyes twinkling in the twilight. Zach looked utterly gorgeous dressed casually in blue denim jeans and a light blue cotton shirt that was rolled up to his forearms. The colour of his shirt intensified the blue rim in his grey eyes and the deep tan of his skin.

Her stomach gave a little flutter when he sent her a quick smile. He was so devastatingly attractive when he lost that grim look. The line of his jaw was still firm, he was too masculine for it ever to be described as anything but determined, but his mouth was sensual and sensitive rather than severe, as she had earlier thought.

Her mouth tingled in memory of how those lips had felt against hers. She remembered every moment of that heart-stopping kiss. It was imprinted on her memory like an indelible brand. She wondered if she would spend the rest of her life recalling it, measuring any subsequent kisses by its standard.

He had deftly changed the subject when she had stumblingly tried to explain her actions of the other night. He had given an apology of sorts for kissing her, but he hadn't said he wasn't going to do it again. She was not by any means a vain person but she was woman enough to know when a man showed an interest in her. He might be able to keep his expression masked and his emotions under lock and key but she had still sensed it.

She had *felt* it in his touch.

She had *tasted* it in his kiss.

She sensed it now as he handed her the glass of wine she had left behind. His eyes held hers for a little longer than they needed to, something passing in the exchange that was unspoken but no less real. She tried to avoid touching his fingers this time. It was increasingly difficult to disguise the way she reacted to him. Would any other man stir her senses quite the way he did? Her body seemed to have a mind of its own when he came near. It was like stepping inside the pull of a powerful magnet. She felt the tug in her flesh, the entire surface of her skin stretching, swelling to get closer to him.

'Thanks.' She took a careful sip of wine. 'Mmm... lovely. Is that a local one?'

He showed her the label. 'It's from a boutique vineyard a couple of hundred kilometres away. I went to boarding school with the guy who owns it.'

'How old were you when you went to boarding school?'

'Eleven.' He swirled the wine in his glass, watching as it splashed around the sides with an almost fierce concentration. 'It was the year after my mother left.' He raised the glass and took a mouthful, the strong column of his throat moving as he swallowed deeply.

'Were you dreadfully homesick?'

He glanced at her briefly before looking back out over the paddocks that were bathed in a pinkish hue instead of their tired brown. 'Not for long.'

Izzy suspected he had taught himself not to feel anything rather than suffer the pain of separation. Homesickness—like love—would be another emotion he had barred from his repertoire. His iron-strong reserve had come about the hard way—a lifetime of suppressing feelings he didn't want to own. She pictured him as an eleven-year-old, probably tall for his age, broad shouldered, whipcord lean and tanned, and yet inside just a little boy who had desperately missed his mother.

She pushed herself away from the veranda rail where she had been leaning her hip. 'I went to boarding school when I was eight. I cried buckets.'

'Eight is very young.' His voice had a gravelly sound to it and his gaze looked serious and concerned, as if he too was picturing her as a child—that small, inconsolable little pigtailed girl with her collection of Barbie dolls in a little pink suitcase.

'Yes…but somehow I got through it. I haven't got any sisters so the company of the other girls was a bonus.'
Or it was when I met Hannah.

'Any brothers?'

Izzy felt that painful stab to her heart again. It didn't matter how many years went past, it was always the same. She found the question so confronting. It was like asking a first-time mother who had just lost her baby if she was still a mother. 'Not any more…' She swallowed to clear the lump in her throat. 'My brother Jamie died five years ago of sarcoma. He was diagnosed when he was fourteen. He was in remission for twelve years and then it came back.'

'I'm sorry.' The deep gravitas in his voice was strangely soothing.

'He wasn't diagnosed early enough.' She gripped the rails of the veranda so tightly the wood creaked beneath her hands. 'He would've had a better chance if he'd gone to a doctor earlier but he was at boarding school and didn't tell anyone about his symptoms until he came home for the holidays.' She loosened her grip and turned back to look at him. 'I think that's what tortures me most. The thought that he might've been saved.'

His eyes held hers in a silent hold that communicated a depth of understanding she hadn't thought him capable of on first meeting him. His quiet calm was a counterpoint to her inner rage at the cruel punch the fist of fate had given to her family and from which they had never recovered.

'Are your parents still together?'

'Yes, but they probably shouldn't be.' Izzy saw the slight questioning lift of his brow and continued. 'My father's had numerous affairs over the years. Even before Jamie's death. In fact, I think it started soon after Jamie was diagnosed. Mum's always clung to her comfortable life and would never do or say anything to jeopardise it, which is probably why she doesn't understand why I ended things with Richard.'

'Why *did* you break it off with him?'

Izzy looked into his blue-rimmed eyes and wondered if he was one of that increasingly rare breed of men who would take his marriage vows seriously, remaining faithful, loyal and devoted over a lifetime. 'I know this probably sounds ridiculously idealistic, romantic even, but I've always wanted to feel the sort of love that stops you in your tracks. The sort that won't go stale or become boring. The sort of love you just know is your one and only chance at happiness. The sort of love you would give everything up for. I didn't feel that for Richard. It wasn't fair to him to go on any longer pretending I did.'

His top lip lifted in a cynical manner. 'So in amongst all those medical textbooks and journals you've managed to sneak in a few romance novels, have you?'

Izzy could have chosen to be offended by his mockery but instead she gave a guilty laugh. 'One or two.' She toyed with the stem of her glass. 'My friend Hannah thinks I'm a bit of a romance tragic.'

'What did she send you in that package? A stack of sentimental books?'

'If only.' She laughed again to cover her embarrassment. Just as well it was dark enough for him not to see her blush.

'What, then?'

'*Please* don't make me tell you.'

'Come on.' His smile was back and it was just as spine-melting as before. 'You've really got my attention now.'

And you've got mine. 'Promise not to laugh?'

'Promise.'

She let out a breath in a rush. 'A blow-up doll. A male one. I've called him Max.'

He threw his head back and laughed. He had a nice-sounding laugh, rich and deep and genuine, not booming and raucous like Richard's when he'd had one too many red wines.

Izzy gave him a mock glare. 'You promised not to laugh!'

'Sorry.' He didn't look sorry. His lips were still twitching and his eyes twinkled with amusement.

'Hannah thought a stand-in boyfriend would stop me from being lonely. I think I already told you she has a weird sense of humour.'

'Are you going to take him with you when you move on?'

'I'm not sure the Sawyers will appreciate him as part of the furniture.'

'Where do you head after here?' The question was casual. Polite interest. Nothing more.

'Brisbane,' Izzy said. 'I've got a job lined up in a busy GP clinic. After that I have a stint in Darwin. The locum agency is pretty flexible. There's always somewhere needing a doctor, especially out in the bush. That's why I took this post. The guy they had lined up had to pull out at the last minute due to a family crisis. I was happy to step in. I'm enjoying it. Everyone's been lovely.'

Zach absently rubbed the toe of his booted foot against one of the uneven floorboards. 'Everyone, apart from my father.'

'I haven't given up on him.'

The silence hummed as their gazes meshed again.

Izzy's breath hitched on something, like a silk sleeve catching on a prickly bush. She moistened her lips as his gaze lowered to her mouth, her stomach feeling as if a tiny fist had reached through her clothes and clutched at her insides.

Male to female attraction was almost palpable in the air. She could feel it moving through the atmosphere like sonic waves. It spoke to her flesh, calling all the pores of her skin to lift up in a soft carpet of goose-bumps, each hair on her head to stand up and tingle at the roots. A hot wire fizzed in her core, sparking a wave of restless energy unlike anything she had ever felt before. It moved through her body, making her as aware of her erogenous zones as if he had reached out and kissed and caressed each one in turn. Her neck, just below her ears, her décolletage, her breasts, the base of her spine, the backs of her knees, her inner thighs…

His eyes moved from her gaze to her mouth and back again. He seemed to be fighting an internal battle. She could see it being played out on his tightly composed features. Temptation and common sense were waging a war and it seemed he hadn't yet decided whose team he was going to side with.

'Are you still in love with your ex?' It was a question Izzy couldn't stop herself asking. Was a little shocked she had.

The night orchestra beyond the veranda filled the silence for several bars. The percussion section of insects. A chorus of frogs. A lonely solo from a stone curlew.

Izzy found herself holding her breath, hoping he wasn't still in love with his ex-fiancée. Why? She couldn't answer. Didn't want to answer. Wasn't ready to answer.

'No.' The word was final. Decisive. It was as if a line had been drawn in his head and he wasn't going back over it.

'But you were hurt when she ended things?'

He gave her a look she couldn't quite read. 'How did your ex take it when you broke things off?'

'Remarkably well.'

One of his brows lifted. 'Oh?'

'He found a replacement within a matter of days.' Izzy looked at the contents of her glass rather than meet his gaze. 'Don't get me wrong…I didn't want him to be inconsolable or anything, but it was a slap in the face when he found someone so completely the opposite of me and so quickly.'

'Why did you accept his proposal in the first place?' Was that a hint of censure in his tone?

Izzy thought back to the elaborate proposal Richard had set up. A very public proposal that had made her feel hemmed in and claustrophobic. She hadn't had the courage to turn him down and make him lose face in front of all of her friends and colleagues. The banner across the front of the hospital with *Will You Marry Me, Izzy?* emblazoned on it had come has a complete and utter shock to her on arriving at work. She could still see Richard down on bended knee, with the Remington heirloom engagement ring taken out of his family's bank vault especially for the occasion, his face beaming with pride and enthusiasm.

No had been on her tongue but hadn't made it past her embarrassed smile. She'd told herself it was the right thing to do. They'd known each other for years. They'd drifted into casual dating and then into a physical relationship. He had been one of Jamie's close friends and had stuck by him during every gruelling bout of chemo. Her parents adored him. He was part of the family. It was her way of staying connected with her lost brother. 'Lots of reasons.'

'But not love.'

'No.' Izzy let out a breath that felt like she had been holding it inside her chest for years. 'That's why I came out here, as far away from home as possible. I want to know who I am without Richard or my parents telling me what to do and how and when I should do it. My parents have expectations for me. I guess all parents do, but I've got my own life to live. They thought I was wasting my time going to medical school when I have enough money behind me to never have to work. But I want to make a difference in people's lives. I want to be the one who saves someone's brother for them, you know?'

Zach's gaze was steady on hers, his voice low and husky. 'I do know.'

Izzy bit her lip. Had she told him too much? Revealed too much? She put her glass down. 'Sorry. Two sips of wine and I'm spilling all my secret desires.' She gave a mental cringe at her choice of words. 'Maybe I should just leave before I embarrass you as well as myself.'

Zach blocked her escape by placing a hand on her arm. 'What do you think would happen if we followed through on this?'

Her skin sizzled where his hand lay on her arm. She could feel the graze of the rough callus on his fingers, reminding her he was a man in every sense of the word. 'Um…I'm not sure what you mean. Follow through on what?'

His eyes searched hers for a lengthy moment. 'So that's the way you're going to play it. Ignore it. Pretend it's not there.' He gave a little laugh that sounded very deep and very sexy. 'That could work.'

Izzy pressed her lips together, trying to summon up some willpower. Where had it gone? Had she left it behind in England? It certainly wasn't here with her now. 'I think it's for the best, don't you?'

'You reckon you've got what it takes to unlock this banged-up cynical heart of mine, Dr Courtney?' He was mocking her again. She could see it in the way the corner of his mouth was tilted and his eyes glinted at her in the darkness.

She gave him a pert look to disguise how tempted she was to take him on. 'I'm guessing I'd need a lot more than a month, that is if I could be bothered, which I can't.'

He brushed an idle fingertip underneath the base of her upraised chin. 'I would like nothing better right now than to take you inside and show you a good time.'

Izzy suppressed the shiver of longing his light touch evoked. 'What makes you think I'd be interested?'

His gaze moved between each of her eyes. 'Have you slept with anyone since your fiancé?'

'No, but I hardly see how that's got anything to do with anything.'

His fingertip moved like a feather over her lower lip. 'Might explain the fireworks the other night.'

'Just because I got a little excited about a kiss doesn't mean I'm going to jump into bed with you any time soon.' She knew she sounded a little schoolmarmish but she desperately wanted to hide how attracted she was to him. She had never felt such an intensely physical reaction to a man before. His very presence made every nerve in her body pull tight with anticipation.

His tall, firm body was not quite touching hers but was close enough for her to feel the warmth that emanated from him. He planted a hand on the veranda post just above the left side of her head. 'Thing is...' his eyes went to her mouth again '...everyone already thinks I'm doing you.'

A wave of heat coursed through her lower body as his eyes came back to burn into hers. The thought of him 'doing' her made her insides contort with lust. She could picture it in her mind, his body so much bigger and more powerfully made than her ex-fiancé's. Somehow she knew there would be nothing predictable or formulaic about any such encounter. She wouldn't be staring at the ceiling, counting the whorls on the ceiling rose to pass the time. It would be mind-blowing pleasure from start to finish.

'It's just gossip... I'm sure it'll go away once they see there's no truth in it...' If only she could get her voice to sound firm and full of conviction instead of that breathy, phone-sex voice that seemed to be coming out.

'Maybe.'

She saw his nostrils flare as he took in the fragrance of her perfume. She could smell his lemon-based aftershave and his own warm, male smell that was equally intoxicating. She could see the shadow of stubble that peppered his jaw and around his nose and mouth and remembered with another clench of lust how it had felt so sexily abrasive against her skin when he'd kissed her.

A wick of something dangerous lit his gaze. 'Ever had a one-night stand before?'

'No.' She swept her tongue over her lips. 'You?'

'Couple of times.'

'Before or after your fiancée?'

'Before.'

Izzy couldn't drag her gaze away from his mouth. She remembered how it had tasted. How it had felt. The way his firm lips had softened and hardened in turn. The way his tongue had seduced hers. Bewitching her. Giving her a hint of the thorough possession he would take of her if she allowed him. 'So…no one since?' She couldn't believe she was asking such personal questions. It was so unlike her.

'No.' He took a wisp of her hair and curled it around one of his fingers, triggering a sensual tug in her inner core. 'We could do it and get it over with. Defuse the bomb, so to speak.'

She moistened her lips again. She could feel herself wavering on a threshold she had never encountered before. Temptation lured her like a moth towards a light that would surely scorch and destroy. 'You're very confident of yourself, aren't you?'

His gaze had a satirical light as it tussled with hers. 'I recognise lust when I see it.'

Izzy felt the lust she was trying to hide crawl all over her skin, leaving it hot and flushed. She took an uneven breath, shocked at how much she wanted him. It was an ache that throbbed in her womb, prickling and swelling the flesh of her breasts until they felt twice their normal size. 'I'm not the sort of girl who jumps into bed with virtual strangers.' *Even if he was the most attractive and intriguing man she had ever met.*

His eyes held hers for a semitone of silence. 'You know my name. Where I live. What I do for a living. You've even met my father. That hardly makes me a stranger.'

'I don't know your values.'

His mouth kicked up wryly in one corner. 'I'm a cop. Can't get more value-driven than that.'

Izzy gave him an arch look. 'I've met some pretty nasty wolves in cops' clothing in my time.'

His hand was still pressed against the post of the veranda, his strongly muscled arm close enough for her cheek to feel its warmth. His warm breath with its hint of summer wine caressed her face as he spoke in that low, deep, gravel-rough voice. 'I only bat for the good guys.'

Izzy could feel herself melting. Her muscles softened, her ligaments loosened, her hands somehow came up to rest against the hard wall of his chest. His pectoral muscles flinched under the soft press of her palms as if he found her as electrifying as she found him. His eyes were locked on hers, a question burning in their grey-blue depths. An invitation. 'I don't normally do this sort of thing...' Her voice was not her own. It was barely a whisper of sound, and yet it was full of unspoken longing.

His eyes lowered to gaze at her mouth. 'Kiss men you hardly know?'

She looked at his mouth, her belly shifting like a foot stepping on a floating plank. He had a beautiful mouth, sensual and neatly sculpted, the lips neither too thick nor too thin. 'Is that all we're doing? Kissing?'

His gaze became sexily hooded. 'Let's start with that and see where it takes us.'

CHAPTER EIGHT

HIS MOUTH CAME down and covered hers in a kiss that tasted of wine and carefully controlled need. It was a slow kiss, with none of the hot urgency of the other night. This one was more languid, leisurely, a slow but thorough exploration of her mouth that made her pulse skyrocket all the same.

Her heart beat like a drum against her ribcage, her hands moving up his chest to link around his neck. He was much taller than her, so that she had to lift up on her toes, bringing her pelvis into intimate contact with his. The pressure of his kiss intensified, his tongue driving through the seam of her mouth in a commanding search of hers. She felt its sexy rasp, the erotic glide and thrusts that so brazenly imitated the act of human mating. Carnal needs surged like a wild beast in her blood; she felt them do the same in his. The throbbing pulse of his erection pounded against her belly; so thick, so strong, so arrantly male it made her desire race out of her control like a rabid dog slipping its leash.

She pressed herself closer, loving the feel of his chest against her breasts, the way the cotton of his shirt smelt, so clean and laundry fresh with that sexy understory of male body heat.

His tongue played with hers, light and teasing and playful at first, determined and purposeful the next. He drew her closer with a firm, warm hand in the small of her back, the other hand skimming over her right breast, the touch light but devastatingly arousing. Izzy liked it that he hadn't made a grab for her, squeezing too tightly or baring her flesh too quickly. His fainéant touch caused a sensual riot in her body, making her ache to feel his calloused palm on her soft skin. She made a murmur of assent against his mouth, reaching for his hand and bringing it back to the swell of her breast. He cupped her through her clothes; his large palm should have made her feel inadequately small but never had she felt more feminine.

His mouth moved down from hers, along the line of her jaw, lingering at the base of her ear where every sensitive nerve shrieked in delight as his tongue laved her flesh. 'You like that?' His voice came from deep within him, throaty, husky.

She sighed with pleasure. 'Hate it.'

He gave a little rumble of laughter as his lips moved to her collarbone. 'Let's see how much you hate this, then.' His hand released the zipper on the back of her dress just enough to uncover one of her shoulders. The feel of his lips and tongue on the cap of her shoulder made her spine soften like candlewax. For a man who hadn't had sex in a while he certainly hadn't lost his touch. Izzy had never been subjected to such a potent assault on her senses. Her body was a tingling matrix of over stimulated nerves, each one screaming out for assuagement.

He moved from her shoulder to the upper curve of her breast showing above her lowered dress. His lips left a quicksilver trail of fire over her flesh, causing her to whimper as the need tightened and pulled inside her.

He tugged her dress a little lower, not bothering to unclip her bra; he simply moved it out of his way and closed his mouth over her tightly budded nipple. The moist warmth of his mouth, the graze of his teeth and the salve of his tongue as he nipped and licked and sucked her in turn made her shudder with pleasure.

Izzy splayed her fingers through the thickness of his hair, holding him to her, prolonging the delicious sensations for as long as she could. His hand on the small of her back moved around her body to possess her hip. It was a strong alpha type of hold that thrilled her senses into overload. Her inner core moistened as he brought her hard against him.

He left her breast to lick the scaffold of her collarbone in one sexy sweep of his tongue. 'We should stop.'

'W-we should?' Izzy had to remind her good girl to get back inside her head and her body. 'Yes. Right. Of course we should.' She pulled her dress back up over her shoulder but she couldn't quite manage the zip with her fumbling fingers.

He turned her so her back was towards him, his fingers an electric shock against her skin as he dragged the zipper back up. His body brushed hers from behind, his hands coming to rest on the tops of her shoulders as if he couldn't quite bring himself to release her just yet. The temptation to lean back against his arousal, to feel him probe her in that sinfully erotic fashion was overwhelming. Just the thought of him there, so close, so thick and turgid with want, was enough to make her flesh hot all over.

'Um…you can let me go now.' Her voice was still that whisper-soft thread of sound.

His hands tightened for the briefest of moments before they fell away. He stepped back, the floorboards of the veranda creaking in protest as if they too felt her disappointment. 'You want a top-up of your drink before dinner?'

Izzy couldn't believe how even his tone was, so cool and calm and collected as if his senses hadn't been subjected to the biggest shake-up of all time. 'I'd better not. What I've had so far seems to have gone straight to my head.'

Even though most of his face was in shadow she caught a glimpse of a half-smile before he turned and went back to the kitchen to see to their meal.

Izzy looked at Popeye, who was looking up at her with bright button eyes. 'Don't look at me like that. I wasn't going to do it. I'm not a one-night stand sort of girl.'

Popeye barked and then jumped off the cane chair and trotted after his master.

Zach planted his hands on the kitchen bench and drew in a long, slow breath to steady himself. It had been a long time since he had let hot-blooded passion overrule common sense. That was the stuff of teenage hormones, not of a thirty-three-year-old man who had responsibilities and priorities.

But, damn it, Izzy Courtney was tempting. His body was thrumming with need, his mouth still savouring the sweetness of hers. Was he asking for trouble to indulge in a fling with her while she was here? It wasn't as if either of them would be making any promises.

She had an end point in sight. She had plans. Commitments elsewhere. He had responsibilities he couldn't leave. Wouldn't leave.

The trouble was he liked her. Not just sexual attraction. He actually *liked* her. She was intelligent, hard-working, committed to serving the community. Everyone was talking about how well she was fitting in. He hadn't heard a bad said word about her.

Zach heard the sound of a mobile phone ringing. He glanced at his phone lying on the bench but the screen was dark. He wasn't on duty tonight, Rob Heywood was.

Izzy came in from the veranda with an apologetic look on her face. 'I'm sorry, Zach. I have to leave. Caitlin Graham's little girl Skylar has fallen off a bed while playing with her older brothers and cut her forehead. It might not be much but with little kids you can never be sure. I'm going to meet them at the clinic.'

Zach snatched up his keys. 'I'll drive down with you.'

'But I've only had a couple of sips of wine.'

'It's not that. We can take both cars.' He turned off the oven on his way past. 'Caitlyn's new boyfriend, Wayne Brody, is a bit of a hot head, especially if he's been drinking.'

Izzy's eyes widened. 'Are you saying Skylar might not have fallen out of bed?'

Zach kept his expression cop neutral. 'Best we take a look at the evidence first.'

Zach and Izzy arrived at the clinic just as a young woman in her early to mid-twenties was getting out of a car that looked like it could do with a makeover. But then, Caitlyn Graham looked the same. Her skin was weathered by a combination of harsh sun and years of smoking, the tell-tale stain of nicotine on her fingers mirroring the rust on her car, her mouth downturned at the edges as if there wasn't much in her life to smile about. There was no sign of the boyfriend Zach had mentioned, which made Izzy wonder if what he had alluded to had any grounds in truth. Caitlyn carried a whimpering two-year-old girl in her arms and two little boys of about five and seven trailed in her wake, the younger one sucking his thumb, the older one carrying a toy dinosaur.

'I'm sorry to drag you out but I think she needs stitches,' Caitlin said, hitching her daughter to her other bony hip as she took the five-year-old's hand. The little girl buried her head against her mother's thin chest and gave another mewling cry.

'Let's go inside and take a look.' Izzy smiled at the boys. 'Hi, guys. Wow, that's a nice triceratops.'

The seven-year-old gave her a scornful look from beneath long spider leg eyelashes. 'It's a stegosaurus.'

'Oh, right. My mistake.' Izzy caught Zach's glinting glance as she led the way into the clinic.

On examination little Skylar had a gash on her forehead that had stopped bleeding due to the compress her mother had placed on it but still needed a couple of stitches to ensure it healed neatly. There were no other injuries that she could see and the child otherwise seemed in good health.

'I'll put some anaesthetic cream on her forehead before I inject some local,' Izzy said to Caitlyn. 'It'll still sting a bit but hopefully not too much.'

Once the stitches were in place, Izzy handed the little tot a choice of the lollipops she kept in a jar on her desk. 'What a brave little girl you've been.'

The little girl chose a red one and silently handed it to her mother to take the cellophane wrapping off.

'Can I have one too?' the five-year-old, called Eli, asked around his thumb.

'Of course. Here you go.' Izzy then passed the jar to the seven-year-old with the stegosaurus. The boy hesitated before finally burying his hand in the jar and taking out two lollipops.

'Only one, Jobe,' Caitlyn said.

The boy gave his mother a defiant look. 'I'm taking one for Dad.'

Caitlyn's lips tightened. 'It'll be stale before you see him again.'

Izzy watched as Jobe's dark eyes hardened. It was a little shocking to see such a young child exhibiting such depth of emotion. Not childlike emotion but emotion well beyond his years. 'I'd like to see Skylar in a couple of days to check those stitches,' she said to defuse the tense atmosphere. 'If it's tricky getting into town, I can always make a house call.'

'I can get here no trouble.'

Was it her imagination or had Caitlin been a little bit too insistent? Izzy shook off the thought. Zach's comments earlier had made her unnecessarily biased. Not every stepfather was a child abuser. Jobe was a tense child but that was probably because he missed his biological father, who apparently was no longer on the scene. 'Let's make an appointment now.' She reached for the computer mouse to bring up the clinic's electronic diary.

'I'll call Margie tomorrow,' Caitlin said. 'I'd better get back. My partner will wonder what's happened.'

'You can use the phone here if you like.'

Caitlyn was already at the door. 'Come on, boys. It's way past your bedtime.'

Jobe was looking at Zach with an intense look on his face. 'Do you always carry a gun?'

'Not always,' Zach said. 'Only when I'm on duty.'

'Are you on duty now?'

'No. Sergeant Heywood is.'

'What if a bad guy came to your house? Would you be allowed to shoot him if you're not on duty?'

Caitlyn came back over and grabbed Jobe by the back of his T-shirt. 'Come on. Sergeant Fletcher's got better things to do than answer your dumb questions.'

The little boy shrugged off his mother's hand and scowled. 'They're not dumb.'

'Don't answer back or I'll give you a clip across the ear.'

Zach crouched down to Jobe's level. 'Maybe you and your brother could drop into the station one day and have a look around. I can show you how the radio works and other cool stuff.' He glanced up at Caitlyn. 'That all right with you?'

Caitlyn's mouth was so tight her lips were white. 'Sure. Whatever.'

Izzy chewed at her lower lip as she began to tidy up the treatment area. Zach came back in from seeing the young family out to the car. She turned and looked at him. 'Cute kids.'

He was frowning in a distracted manner. 'Yeah.'

'You think she would hit Jobe or the other two?'

'A lot of parents do. It's called discipline.'

'There are much better ways to discipline a child than to hit them,' Izzy said. 'How can you teach a child not to hit others if you're hitting them yourself?'

'You're preaching to the choir,' he said. 'I don't agree with it either but some parents insist it's their right to use corporal punishment.'

'I didn't notice any bruises or marks on the little one but Jobe seems a very tense little boy. He doesn't seem to have a close relationship with his mother, does he?'

'He misses his dad.'

'Where is he?'

He shrugged. 'Who knows? Probably shacked up with some other woman with another brood of kids by now.'

Izzy washed her hands at the sink and then tore off a paper towel to dry them. 'Beats me why some people have kids if they're just going to abandon them when the going gets tough.'

'Tell me about it.'

She looked at him again. 'Did your mother remarry?'

'Yes. Got a couple of sons. They take up a lot of her time.'

'I'm sorry…I shouldn't have asked.'

'It was a long time ago.'

She put the used paper towel in the pedal bin. 'Do you want kids?' *Where on earth had that question come from?* 'Sorry.' She bit her lip again. 'None of my business.'

'I do, actually.' He picked up a drug company's promotional paperweight off her desk and smoothed his right thumb over its surface. 'Not right now, though.

Maybe in a couple of years or so. I have to get a few things straightened out first.'

'Your father?'

He put the paperweight down and met her gaze. 'It's a good sign he went out tonight.'

'Yes, I agree. Social isolation isn't good for someone suffering depression.'

There was a little silence.

'What about you?' he asked. 'Do you want kids or is your career your top priority?'

'I would hate to miss out on having a family. I love my career but I really want to be a mum one day.'

It was hard to tell if her answer met with his approval or not. He had his cop face on again. 'Caitlyn Graham had Jobe when she was fifteen. She was a kid with a kid.'

'It looks like she's had it tough,' Izzy said. 'Do all three kids have the same father?'

'No, Eli and Skylar are another guy's. A drifter who came into town for a couple of years before moving on again.'

'Does Caitlyn have any extended family to support her?'

'Her mother comes to visit from Nyngan now and again but she never stays long.' His mouth took on a cynical line. 'Just long enough to have a fight with Caitlyn's new boyfriend.'

'He doesn't sound like a good role model for the boys,' Izzy said.

He gave her a grim look. 'He's not. He's been inside for assault and possession and supply of illegal drugs. He's only just come off parole. Reckon it won't be long before he ends up back behind bars.'

'Once a criminal, always a criminal?'

'In my experience, most of the leopards I've met like to hang onto their spots.'

'Don't you think people can change if they're given some direction and support?' Izzy asked.

'Maybe some.'

She picked up her bag and hitched it over her shoulder. 'Were you always this cynical or has your job made you that way?'

He held the door open for her. 'I'll tell you over dinner.'

'You still want me to—?'

His look was unreadable. 'You're still hungry, aren't you?'

Izzy had a feeling he wasn't just talking about food. 'It's getting late. Maybe I should just head home. Your dad will be back soon in any case.'

'If that's what you want.' He sounded as if he didn't care either way.

It wasn't what she wanted but she wasn't quite ready to admit it. She wasn't sure how to handle someone as deep and complicated as Zach Fletcher. He was strong and principled, almost to the point of being conservative, which, funnily enough, resonated with her own homespun values. But she was only here for another three weeks. It wouldn't be fair to start something she had no intention of finishing. 'Thanks for coming down with me to see to little Skylar.'

'You'd better get Margie to give Caitlyn a call tomorrow. She's not good at following through on stuff.'

'Yes, I gathered that.'

Once she had locked the clinic and set the alarm, Zach walked her to her car. He waited until she was inside the car with her seat belt pulled down and clipped into place.

'Thanks again.'

He tapped the roof of her car with his hand. 'Drive safely.'

'Zach?'

He stopped and turned back to look at her. 'Yes?'

'Maybe I could cook dinner for you some time…to make up for tonight?'

He gave her the briefest of smiles. 'I'll get working on my appetite.'

CHAPTER NINE

'HOW DID YOUR evening go with Doug Fletcher?' Izzy asked Margie the next morning at the clinic.

'I was about to ask you the same question about yours with Zach.'

'It got cut short. I got called out to Caitlyn Graham's little daughter, who'd cut her forehead,' Izzy said. 'Can you call her to make a follow-up appointment? I'd like to see Skylar on Thursday. And can you check to see whether all three kids are up to date on their vaccinations?'

'Will do. Did Caitlyn's boyfriend come with her?'

'No, but Zach warned me about him. He came with me to the clinic.'

Margie's brows lifted. 'Did he, now?'

Izzy felt a blush creep over her cheeks. 'He's a bit of a stickler for safety.'

'Wayne Brody is a ticking time bomb,' Margie said. 'Wouldn't take much to set him off. Zach's got a good nose for sensing trouble.'

'Why would Caitlyn hook up with someone so unsavoury? There must be some other much nicer young man out here.'

Margie shrugged. 'Some girls would rather be with

anybody rather than nobody. Her mother's the same. Hooked up with one deadbeat after the other. I don't think Caitlyn has ever met her biological father. I'm not sure her mother even knows who it is. Caitlyn had one stepfather after the other. Now she's doing the same to her kids. It's a cycle that goes on one generation after another. It's a case of monkey see, monkey do.'

'Are there any playgroups or activities for young mums like her around here?' Izzy asked.

'Peggy McLeod tried to set one up a few years back but her arthritis set in and she had to give it up. No one's bothered to do anything since.'

'The community centre...do you think I could book it for one morning this week?' Izzy asked. 'I could re-arrange my clinic hours. I could get some toys donated or buy them myself if I have to. It'd be a place for the mums and kids to hang out and chat and play.'

'Sounds good, but who's going to take over when your time with us is up?'

'I could get one of the mums to take charge,' Izzy said. 'It might be a chance to get Caitlyn engaged in something that would build her self-esteem.'

Margie gave a snort. 'There's nothing wrong with that girl's self-esteem. It's her taste in men that's the problem.'

'But that's exactly my point,' Izzy said. 'She thinks so badly of herself that she settles for the first person who shows an interest in her. There's a saying I heard once. You get the partner in life you think you deserve.'

Margie gave her a twinkling look. 'And who do you think you deserve?'

Izzy felt that betraying blush sneak back into her

cheeks. 'Did you manage to convince Doug to book in for a check-up?'

Margie's twinkle dulled like a cloud passing over the sun. 'I'm working on it.'

'Are you going to see him again?'

'I'm working on that too,' Margie said. 'I mentioned the Shearers' Ball but he was pretty adamant he wasn't going to go.'

'I guess it's pretty hard to dance when you're on a walking frame.'

'It's not about the dancing.' Margie's eyes suddenly watered up. 'I couldn't give a toss about the dancing. I just want to be with him. I've waited so long for him but he's got this stupid idea in his head that no one could ever want him the way he is now.'

Izzy gave Margie's shoulder a gentle squeeze. 'I hope it works out for you and him. I really do.'

Margie popped a tissue out of the box on the reception counter and blew her nose. She tossed the tissue in the bin under the desk and assembled her features back into brisk receptionist mode. 'Silly fool. A woman of my age fancying herself in love. Phhfft. Ridiculous.'

'It's not ridiculous,' Izzy said. 'Falling in love isn't something you can control. It just happens—' she caught Margie's look '—or so I'm told,' she added quickly. She took the file for her first patient of the day from the counter as the front door of the clinic opened. 'Mrs Honeywell? Come this way.'

Zach was leaving the station a couple of days later when he saw Izzy coming out of the clinic and walking towards her car. It had been a brute of a day, hot and dry with a northerly wind that was gritty and relentless.

He could think of nothing better than a cool beer and a swim out at Blake's waterhole… Actually, he could think of something way better than that. Izzy Courtney lying naked underneath him while he—

She suddenly turned and looked at him as if she had felt his gaze on her. Or read his X-rated thoughts. 'Oh…hello.' She gave him a smile that looked beaten up around the edges.

'You look like you've had a tough day.'

Her mouth twisted as she scraped a few tendrils of sticky hair back behind her ear. 'Caitlyn didn't show up for Skylar's check-up. Margie confirmed it with her but she didn't come. I called her on the phone to offer to go out there but there was no answer.' She blew out a little breath of frustration. 'I can't force her to bring the child in. And I don't want to turn up at her house as if I'm suspicious of her.'

'I've got a couple of things for Jobe and Eli,' Zach said. 'Stuff I had when I was a kid. I found them in a cupboard in one of the spare rooms at home. We can drop them round now just to see if everything's OK. Better take your car, though. Might not get such a warm welcome, turning up in mine.'

Her caramel-brown eyes brightened. 'That was thoughtful of you. What sort of things? Toys?'

Zach found himself trying to disguise a sheepish look. 'I went through a dinosaur stage when I was about seven or eight. Got a bit obsessive there for a bit.'

She gave him a smile that loosened some of the tight barbed wire wrapped around his heart. 'So you can tell a stegosaurus from a triceratops?'

'Any fool can do that.'

She pursed her lips and then must have realised he

was teasing her for her sunny smile broke free again. 'You're a nice man, Sergeant Fletcher. I think I'm starting to like you after all.'

The house Caitlyn Graham was living in was on the outskirts of Jerringa Ridge. It was a stockman's cottage from the old days that looked like it hadn't had much done to it since. The rusty gate was hanging on one hinge and the once white but now grey picket fence had so many gaps it looked like a rotten-toothed smile. A dog of mixed breeding was chained near the tank stand and let out a volley of ferocious barking as Izzy pulled her car up in front of the house. 'Can he get off, do you think?' she asked, casting Zach a worried glance.

'I'll keep an eye on him.'

'Poor dog tied up like that in this heat.' She turned off the engine and unclipped her belt. 'Is anyone around? There's no car about that I can see.'

'Stay in the car and I'll have a mosey around.' Zach got out and closed the door with a snick. The dog put its ears back and brought its body low to the ground as it snarled and bared its teeth.

Izzy watched as Zach ignored the dog as he walked up the two steps of the bull-nosed veranda, opening the screen door to knock on the cracked paint of the front door. The dog was still doing its scary impersonation of an alien beast from a horror movie but Zach didn't seem the least put off by it. He left the bag of toys near the door and came back down the veranda steps. Apart from the dinosaurs, Izzy had spotted a set of toy cars and a doll that looked suspiciously new. She had seen one just like it in the corner store yesterday but it hadn't been there when she'd picked up her sandwich today at lunchtime.

Zach made a clicking sound with his tongue and the dog stopped growling and slunk down in a submissive pose. Zach picked up the dog's water dish, took it over to the tap on the base of the tank, rinsed the rusty water out of it and filled it with fresh, setting it down in a patch of shade next to the dog's kennel. The dog drank thirstily, so thirstily Zach had to refill the dish a couple of times.

He came back to the car after doing another round of the house. 'No one home.'

Izzy started the engine. 'You certainly have a way with wild animals.'

'He's not wild.' He leaned his arm along the back of her seat as she backed the car to turn around. 'He's scared. Probably had the boot kicked into his ribs a few too many times.'

Izzy could see the tightness around his jaw. That grim look was back. The look that was like a screen behind which the horrors and cruelty and brutal inhumanity he'd seen first hand were barricaded. 'How do you cope with it? The stuff you see, I mean. The bad stuff.'

'Reckon you've seen your share of bad stuff too.'

'Yes, but I'm not usually out on the coalface. Most of the stuff I see is in the controlled environment of a clinic or hospital. And mostly it's stuff I can fix.'

He didn't speak until Izzy had driven back to the road leading to town. 'It doesn't get any easier, that's for sure. Rocking up to someone's place to tell them their only kid is lying in the morgue after a high-speed accident is the kind of stuff that gets to even the toughest cops.' He paused for a beat. 'Anything to do with kids gets me. Abuse. Neglect. Murder. It's not something you can file away like the investigation report. It stays with you. For years.' He released a jagged breath. 'For ever.'

Izzy glanced at him. 'Did you think it would be as bad as it is when you first joined the force?'

He gave her a twisted smile that had nothing to do with humour. 'Most cops fresh out of the academy think they're going to be the one that changes the world. We all think we're going to make a difference. To help people. Trouble is, some people don't want to be helped.'

'I've been talking to Margie about setting up a playgroup in town,' Izzy said, 'for mums like Caitlyn and their kids. A place to hang out and chat and swap recipes and stuff. Do you think it's a good idea?'

'Who's going to run it?'

'I will, to start with.'

He flashed her an unreadable look. 'And who's going to take over when you drive off into the sunset in search of your next big adventure?'

Izzy pressed her lips together. Was he mocking her or was he thinking of the locals getting all excited about something only to have it fall flat once she left? A little flag of hope climbed up the flagpole of her heart. Was he thinking of how *he* would feel when she left? 'I'm going to be here long enough to get it up and running. After that it's up to the locals to keep things going, if that's what they want.'

He gave a noncommittal grunt, his eyes trained on the road ahead.

Izzy let a silence pass before she added, 'So what's wrong with looking for adventure?'

'Nothing, as long as you don't hurt others going in search of it.'

'I'm not planning on hurting anyone.' She found her fingers tightening on the steering-wheel and had to force herself to relax them. 'I suppose this attitude of yours is because of your mother leaving the way she did.'

She felt the razor-sharp blade of his gaze. 'You really think you've got what it takes to make a difference out here in a month? You haven't got a hope, sweetheart.'

'Don't patronise me by calling me sweetheart.'

He gave a sound midway between a laugh and a cynical snort. 'You flounce into town, sprinkling your fairy dust around, hoping some of it will stick, but you haven't got a clue. The country out here is tough and it needs tough people to work in it and survive. It's not the place for some pretty little blow-in who's looking for something to laugh about over a latte with her friends when she gets back from her big adventure with the rednecks in the antipodes.'

Izzy tried to rein in her anger but it was like trying to control a scrub fire with an eyedropper. The one thing she hated the most was people not taking her seriously. Thinking she was too much of a flake to get the job done. A silly little socialite playing at doctors and nurses. 'Thanks for the charming summation of my motives and character,' she said through tight lips.

'Pleasure.'

She pulled up outside the police station a few bristling minutes later. 'Have a nice evening, Sergeant,' she said, her voice dripping with sarcasm.

He didn't even bother replying, or at least not verbally. He shut the car door with a sharp click that could just as easily be substituted for an imprecation.

* * *

'What's got under your skin?' Doug asked Zach over dinner later that evening. 'You've been stabbing at that steak as if it's a mortal enemy.'

Zach pushed his plate away. 'It's too hot to eat.'

'Tell me about it.' Doug wiped the back of his hand over his forehead. 'Must be something wrong with the air-con. I'm sweating like a pig.'

Zach frowned as he saw his father's sickly colour. 'You all right?'

'Will be in a minute…' Doug gripped the arms of the standard chair. 'Just a funny turn. Had one earlier… just before you got home.'

'When was the last time you took a painkiller?'

'Ran out last night.'

Zach swore under his breath. 'You're not supposed to stop them cold turkey. You're supposed to wean yourself off them. You're probably having withdrawal symptoms. It can be dangerous to suddenly stop taking them.'

Doug winced as he pushed back from the table. 'Maybe you should call the doctor for me. Pain's pretty bad…' He sucked in a breath. 'Getting worse by the minute.'

Zach mentally rolled his eyes as he reached for his phone. The one time he wanted some distance from Izzy Courtney and his father springs a turnaround on him. He considered waiting it out to see if his father recovered without intervention but he knew he would never forgive himself if things took a turn for the worse. His father's health hadn't been checked since William Sawyer had left on holidays. He was supposed to be monitored weekly for his blood pressure. Severe pain could trigger heart attacks in some patients and the last thing Zach wanted was to be responsible for inaction just because of a silly little tiff with the locum doctor.

He was annoyed with himself for reacting the way he had. He didn't want Izzy thinking she had any hold over him. So what if she wanted to get a playgroup going before she left? It was a good idea—a *great* idea. It was exactly what the town needed. She was doing all she could in the short time she was here to make a difference. Once she was done waving her magic wand around he would wave her off without a flicker of emotion showing on his face.

That was one lesson he had learned and learned well.

Izzy arrived twenty-five minutes later, carrying her doctor's bag and a coolly distant manner Zach knew he probably deserved. 'He's in the bedroom, lying down,' he said.

'How long has he been feeling unwell?'

'Since before I got home. He's run out of pain meds. It's probably withdrawal.'

'Is he happy to see me?'

He inched up the corner of his mouth in a sardonic curl. 'You think I would've called you otherwise?'

Her brown eyes flashed a little arc of lightning at him. 'Lead the way.'

Zach knew he was acting like a prize jerk. He couldn't seem to help it. It was the only way to keep his distance. He was worried about complicating his life with a dalliance with her even though he could think of nothing he wanted more than to lose himself in a bit of mindless sex. He didn't have her pegged as the sort of girl who would settle for a fling. She'd been engaged to the same man for four years. That didn't sound like a girl who was eager to put out to the first guy who showed an interest in her.

And Zach was more than interested in her.

He couldn't stop thinking about her. How she'd felt in his arms, the way her mouth had met the passion of his, the softness of her breast in his mouth, the hard little pebble of her nipple against his tongue, the taste of the skin of her neck, that sweet, flowery scent of her that reminded him of an English cottage garden in spring.

'Hello, Mr Fletcher.' Izzy's voice broke through Zach's erotic reverie. 'Zach told me you're not feeling so good this evening.'

'Pain...' Doug gestured to his abdomen and his back; his breathing was ragged now, his brow sticky with sweat. 'Bad pain...'

Zach watched as she examined his father's chest and abdomen and then his back with gentle hands. He couldn't help feeling a little jealous. He would have liked those soft little hands running over his chest and abdomen and lower. His groin swelled at the thought and he had to think of something unpleasant to get control again.

She took his father's blood pressure, her forehead puckered in concentration as she listened to his account of how he had been feeling over the last few hours.

'Any history of renal colic?' she asked. 'Kidney stones?'

'A few years back,' his father said. 'Six or seven years ago, I think. Didn't need to go to hospital or anything. I passed them eventually. Hurt like the devil. None since.'

'I'll give you a shot of morphine for the pain but I think we should organise an IVP tomorrow if the pain doesn't go away overnight,' Izzy said. 'When was the last time you passed urine?'

'Not for a while, three hours ago maybe.'

'Any pain or difficulty?'

'A bit.'

'Do you think you could give me a urine sample if I leave you with a specimen bottle?' she asked as she administered the injection.

'I'll give it a try.'

'I'll wait in the kitchen to give you some privacy.' She clipped shut her bag and walked past Zach, her body brushing his in the doorway making him go hard all over again.

'Might need a hand getting to the bathroom, Zach,' his father said.

Zach blinked a couple of times to reorient himself. 'Right. Sure.'

CHAPTER TEN

IZZY WAS SITTING on one of the kitchen chairs with Popeye on her lap when Zach came back in, carrying a urine sample bottle inside the press-lock plastic bag she'd provided. She put the dog on the floor and stood, taking the sample from him and giving it a quick check for blood or cloudiness that would suggest infection, before putting it next to her bag on the floor.

She straightened and kept her doctor face in place, trying to ignore the way her body was so acutely aware of the proximity of Zach's. 'Your father should be feeling a little better in the next half-hour or so. Make sure he drinks plenty of clear fluids over the next twenty-four hours. If he has any trouble passing urine, don't hesitate to call. If the bladder blocks I can insert a catheter to drain it until we can get him to hospital. But I don't think it will come to that. It seems a pretty standard case of renal colic. Being less active, he probably doesn't feel as thirsty as much as he used to. Older men often fail to keep an adequate intake of fluids.' She knew she was talking like a medical textbook but she couldn't seem to stop it. 'That's about it. I'll be on my way. Goodbye.'

'Izzy.' His hand was firm and warm on the bare skin of her arm. It sent a current of electricity to the secret heart of her.

Izzy met his gaze. It wasn't hard and cold with anger now but tired, as if he had grown weary of screening his inner turmoil from view. Her heart stepped off its high horse and nestled back down in her chest with a soft little sign. 'Are you OK?'

His mouth softened its grim line. 'Sorry about this afternoon. I was acting like a jerk.' His thumb started stroking the skin of her arm, a back-and-forth motion that was drugging her senses.

'You've got a lot on your mind right now with your dad and everything.'

'Don't make excuses for me.' His thumb moved to the back of her hand, absently moving over the tendons in a circular motion. 'I was out of line, snapping your head off like that.'

Izzy gave him a mock reproachful arch of her brow. 'Fairy dust?'

His thumb stalled on her hand and he looked down at it as if he'd only just realised he'd been stroking it. He released her and took a step backwards, using the same hand to score a crooked pathway through his hair. 'Thanks for coming out. I appreciate it. I think you've won my dad over.'

What about you? Have I won you over? Izzy studied his now closed-off expression. 'I hope he has a settled night. Call me if you're worried. I'll keep my phone on.'

He walked her out to the car but he hardly said a word. Izzy got the impression he couldn't wait for her to leave. It made her spirits plummet. She'd thought for a moment back there he'd been going to kiss her, maybe even take it a step further.

She hadn't realised how much she wanted him to until he hadn't.

Caitlyn Graham turned up at the clinic the following day with Skylar. 'Sorry about missing our appointment,' she said. 'I took the kids for a drive to see a friend of mine on a property out of town. I forgot to phone and cancel. There's no signal out there so I couldn't call even when I remembered.'

'No problem,' Izzy said. 'Just as long as Skylar's OK.' She inspected the little tot's forehead and asked casually, 'How are the boys?'

'They're at school,' Caitlyn said. 'Jobe made a fuss about going. He hates it. He has a tantrum about going just about every morning.'

'Is he being bullied?'

'What, at school? Nah, don't think so. Wayne would have a fit if he heard Jobe couldn't stand up for himself.'

'Did you get the bag of toys Zach dropped in for the kids?' Izzy asked.

Caitlyn's expression flickered with something before she got it under control. 'Wayne wasn't too happy about that. He doesn't think it's right to spoil kids, especially if they're not behaving themselves.'

'Does Wayne get on well with the kids?'

'All right, I guess.' Caitlyn brushed her daughter's fluffy blonde hair down into some semblance of order. 'They're not his. None of my kids are.'

'Do you have any contact with Jobe's father?' Izzy asked.

'No, and I don't want to.' Caitlyn's expression tight-

ened like a fist. 'Jobe's got it in his head Connor is some
sort of hero but he's just another loser. Connor caused
a lot of trouble between Brad and me—that's Eli and
Skylar's dad. It's what broke us up, actually.'

'What sort of trouble?'

'Picking fights. Saying things about Brad that
weren't true. Punch-ups on the street. Making me look
like trailer trash. I took a restraining order out on him.
He can't come anywhere near me or Jobe.'

'What about Brad? Does he have contact with Eli
and Skylar?'

'Now and again but Wayne's not keen on it. Thinks
I might be tempted to go back to him or something. As
if.' She rolled her eyes at the thought. 'Wayne's no prize
but at least he brings in a bit of money.'

'What does he do?'

'He's a truck driver. He does four runs a week, sometimes more. He's the first man I've had who's held down
a regular job.'

'It must get lonely out here for you with him away
a lot,' Izzy said.

'It's no picnic with three kids, but, as my mum keeps
saying, I made my bed so I have to lie in it.'

Izzy brought up the subject of a playgroup at the
community centre. Caitlyn shrugged as if the thought
held little appeal but Izzy knew apathy was a common trait amongst young women who felt the world
was against them. 'I'll let you know once we get things
sorted,' she said as Caitlyn left the consulting room.
'Skylar will enjoy it and we might even be able to do
an after-school one if things go well so the boys can
come too.'

'I'll think about it. See what Wayne says. I like to fit in with him. Causes less trouble that way.'

Izzy closed the door once Caitlyn had left. It was a shock to realise she had no right to criticise Caitlyn for accommodating her partner's unreasonable demands.

Hadn't she done more or less the same with Richard for the last four years?

Margie put the reception phone down just as Izzy came out of her room. 'That was Doug Fletcher. He passed a couple of kidney stones last night. He's feeling much better.'

'I'm glad to hear it.'

'Not only that,' Margie continued with a beaming smile, 'he asked me to go over there tonight. I'm going to make him dinner.'

'That's lovely. I'm pleased for you.'

'I have a favour to ask.'

'You want to leave early?' Izzy asked. 'Sure. I can do the filing and lock up.'

'No, not that.' Margie gave her a beseeching look. 'Would you be a honey and invite Zach to dinner at your place tonight?'

'Um…'

'Go on. He'll feel like a gooseberry hanging around with us oldies,' Margie said. 'A night out at your place will be good for him. It'll give him a break from always having to keep an eye on his dad.'

'I don't know…'

'Or ask him to join you for a counter meal at the pub if you're not much of a cook.'

'I can cook.'

'Then what's the problem?'

Izzy schooled her features into what she hoped

passed for mild enthusiasm. 'I'll give him a call. See what he's up to. He might be on duty.'

'He's not. I already checked.'

Zach was typing a follow-up email to his commander in Bourke when Izzy came into the station. He pressed 'Send' and got to his feet. 'I was going to call you. My dad's feeling a lot better.'

'Yes, Margie told me. He called the clinic earlier this morning.'

'You were spot on with your diagnosis.'

'I may not know a triceratops from a stegosaurus but I'm a whizz at picking up renal colic.'

Zach felt a smile tug at his mouth. 'You doing anything tonight?'

She gave him a wry look. 'Apparently I'm cooking dinner for you.'

'Yeah, so I heard. You OK with that?'

'Have I got a choice?'

Zach found it cute the way she arched her left eyebrow in that haughty manner. 'I wouldn't want to put you to any trouble. I can pick up a bite to eat at the pub. Mike hates it when I do, though. He says it puts his regulars off.'

'You don't have to go in uniform.'

'Wouldn't make a bit of difference if I went in stark naked.'

Her cheeks lit up like twin fires. 'Um…dinner's at seven.'

'I'll look forward to it.' She was at the door when he asked, 'Hey, will your stand-in boyfriend Max be joining us?'

She gave him a slitted look over her shoulder and then flounced out.

* * *

Izzy had cooked for numerous dinner parties for her friends when living in London and she'd never felt the slightest hint of nerves. She was an accomplished cook; she'd made it her business to learn as she'd grown up with cooks at Courtney Manor and wasn't content to sit back and watch, like her parents, while someone else did all the work. From a young age she had taken an interest in preparing food, getting to know the kitchen staff and talking to the gardeners about growing fresh vegetables and herbs.

But preparing a meal for Zach in an Outback town that had only one shop with limited fresh supplies was a challenge, so too was trying not to think about the fact she was sure that food was not the only thing they would be sharing tonight.

She put the last touches to the table, thinking wistfully of the fragrant roses of Courtney Manor as she placed an odd-looking banksia on the table in a jam jar, the only thing she could in the cottage that was close to a vase.

Izzy looked at Max sitting at the end of the table. It had taken her half an hour to blow him up manually as she didn't have a bicycle pump. He was leaning to one side, his ventriloquist dummy-like eyes staring into space. 'I hope you're going to behave yourself, Max.' *Why are you talking to a blow-up doll?* 'No talking with your mouth full or elbows on the table, OK?'

The doorbell sounded and Izzy quickly smoothed her already smooth hair as she went to answer it. Zach was standing on the porch, wearing an open-necked white shirt with tan-coloured chinos. His hair was still damp from a shower; she could see the grooves where his comb or brush had passed through it. Her first 'Hi...' came out croakily so she cleared her throat and tried again. 'Hi. Come on in.'

'Thanks.'

She could smell the clean fresh scent of fabric softener on his shirt as he came through the door, that and the hint of lemon and spice and Outback maleness that never failed to get her senses spinning.

'I brought wine.' He handed her a bottle, his eyes moving over her in a lazy sweep that made her insides feel hollow. 'Something smells good.'

Izzy took the wine, getting a little shock from his fingers as they brushed against hers. 'I hope you're hungry.'

'Ravenous.'

She swallowed and briskly turned to get the glasses, somehow managing to half fill two without spilling a drop in spite of hands that weren't too steady. 'Max decided to join us after all.' She handed Zach a glass of the white wine he had brought. 'I hope you don't mind.'

A hint of a smile played at the corners of his mouth. 'Aren't you going to introduce us?'

Izzy felt her own smile tug at her lips. 'He's not one for small talk.'

'I'm known to be a bit on the taciturn side myself.' The smile had travelled up to his eyes with a twinkle that was devastatingly attractive.

She led the way to the small eating area off the kitchen. 'Max, this is Sergeant Zach Fletcher.' She turned to Zach. 'Zach, this is Max.'

Zach rubbed at his chin thoughtfully. 'Mmm, I guess a handshake is out of the question?'

A laugh bubbled out of Izzy's mouth. 'This is ridiculous. I'm going to kill Hannah. I swear to God I will. Would you like some nibbles?' she asked as she thrust a plate of dips and crackers towards him. 'I have to check on the entrée.'

His eyes were still smiling but they had taken on a smouldering heat that made the backs of her knees feel tingly. 'Do you think Max would get jealous if I kissed you?'

Izzy's stomach hollowed out again. 'I don't know. I've never kissed anyone in front of him before.'

He put a hand to the side of her face, a gentle cupping of her cheek, the dry warmth and slight roughness of his palm making her inner core quiver like an unset jelly. 'I wouldn't want to cut in on him but I've been dying to do this since last night.' His mouth came down towards hers, his minty breath dancing over the surface of her lips in that tantalising prelude to take-off.

Izzy let out a soft sigh of delight as his mouth connected with hers, a velvet brush of dry male lips on moist, lip-gloss-coated female ones. The moment of contact made shivers flow like a river down her spine, the first electrifying sweep of his tongue over her lips parted them, inviting her to take him in. She opened to the commanding glide of his tongue, shuddering with need as he made contact with hers in a sexy tangle that drove every other thought out of her mind other than what she was feeling in her body. The stirring of her blood, the way her feminine folds pulsed and ached to be parted and filled, just like he was doing with her mouth. The way her breasts tingled and tightened, the nipples erect in arousal.

His hands grasped her by the hips, pulling her against his own arousal, the hard heat of him probing her intimately, reminding her of everything that was different between them and yet so powerfully, irresistibly attractive.

Izzy snaked her arms around his neck, stepping up on her toes so she could keep that magical connection with his mouth on hers. She kissed him with the passion that had been lying dormant inside her body, just waiting for someone like him to awaken it. She had never felt the full force of it before. She'd felt paltry imitations of it, but nothing like this.

This was fiery.

This was unstoppable.

This was inevitable.

'I want you.' Izzy couldn't believe she had said the words out loud, but even if she hadn't done so her body was saying them for her. The way she was clinging to him, draping her body over him like a second layer of skin, was surely leaving him in no doubt of her need for him. She pressed three hot little kisses, one after the other, on his mouth and repeated the words she had never said to anyone else and meant them quite the way she meant them now. 'I want you to make love to me.'

Zach brought his hands back up to cup her face. 'Sure?'

Izzy gazed into his beautiful haunted eyes. 'Don't you recognise consent when you see it?'

His thumbs stroked her cheeks, his eyes focused on her mouth as if it were the most fascinating thing he had ever seen. 'It's been a while for me.'

'I'm sure you still know the moves.'

One of his thumbs brushed over her lower lip in a caress that made the base of her spine shiver. 'Are we having a one-night stand or is this something else?'

'What do you want it to be?'

He took a while to answer, his gaze still homed in on her mouth, the pads of his thumbs doing that mesmerising stroking, one across her cheek, the other on her lower lip. 'You're only here for another couple of weeks. Neither of us is in the position to make promises.'

'I'm not asking for promises,' Izzy said. 'I had promises and they sucked.'

His mouth kicked up at the corner. 'Yeah, me too.'

She placed her fingertip on his bottom lip, caressing it the way he had done to hers. 'I've never had a fling with someone before.'

Something in his gaze smouldered. Simmered. Burned. 'Flings can be fun as long as both parties are clear on the rules.'

Izzy shivered as he took her finger in his mouth, his teeth biting down just firmly enough for her insides to flutter in anticipatory excitement. 'You're mighty big on rules, aren't you, Sergeant? I guess that's because of that gun you're wearing.'

His hands encircled her wrists like handcuffs, his pelvis carnally suggestive against hers. 'I'm not wearing my gun.'

Her brow arched in a sultry fashion. 'Could've fooled me.'

He scooped her up in his arms in an effortless lift, calling out over his shoulder as he carried her towards the bedroom, 'Start without us, Max. We've got some business to see to.'

Izzy quaked with pleasure when Zach slid her down the length of his body once he had her in the bedroom. And there was a *lot* of his body compared to hers. So tall, so lean and yet so powerfully muscled she barely came up to his shoulder once she'd kicked off her heels. His hands cupped her bottom and pulled her against him, letting her feel the weight and heft of his erection. Even through the barrier of their clothes it was the most erotic feeling to have him pulse and pound against her. He kissed her lingeringly, deeply, taking his time to build her need of him until she was whimpering, gasping, clawing at him to get him naked.

'What's the hurry?' he said against the side of her neck.

Izzy kissed his mouth, his chin, and then flicked the tip of her tongue into the dish below his Adam's apple. 'I've heard things go at a much slower pace in the Outback but I didn't realise that included sex.'

He gave a little rumble of laughter and pulled the zipper down the back of her dress in a single lightning-fast movement. 'You want speed, sweetheart?' He unclipped her bra and tossed it to the floor. 'Then let's see if we can pick up the pace a bit, shall we?'

Izzy whooshed out a breath as she landed on her back on the mattress with a little bounce. As quickly as he had removed her clothes, he got rid of his own, coming down over her, gloriously, deliciously naked.

The sexy entanglement of limbs, of long and hard and toned and tanned and hair-roughened muscles entwining with softer, smoother, shorter ones made everything that was feminine in her roll over in delight. His hands, those gorgeously manly hands, sexily grazed the soft skin of her breasts. That sizzling-hot male mouth with its surrounding stubble suckled on each one in turn, the right one first and then the left, the suction just right, the pressure and tug of his teeth perfect, the roll and sweep of his tongue mind-blowing.

Izzy had never been all that vocal during sex in the past. The occasional sigh or murmur perhaps—sometimes just to feed Richard's ego rather than from feeling anything spectacular herself—but nothing like the gasps and whimpers that were coming out of her now. It wasn't just Zach's mouth that was wreaking such havoc on her senses but the feel and shape of his body as it pinned hers to the bed. Not too heavy, not awkward or clumsy, but potent and powerful, determined and yet respectful.

He moved down from her breasts to sear a scorching pathway to her bellybutton and beyond. She automatically tensed when he came to the seam of her body, but immediately sensing her hesitation he placed his palm over her lower abdomen to calm her. 'Trust me, Izzy. I can make it good for you.'

Should she tell him she had never experienced such intimacy before? She didn't want to make Richard sound like a prude, but the truth was he had made it clear early on in their relationship that he found oral sex distasteful. In spite of her knowledge as a doctor to the contrary, his attitude had made her feel as if her body was unpleasant, unattractive and somehow defective. 'Um…I've never done it before… I mean no one's done it to me…'

He looked at her quizzically. 'Your ex didn't?'

She knew she was blushing. But rather than hide it she decided to be honest with him. 'It wasn't Richard's thing.'

He was still frowning. 'But it's one of the best ways for a woman to have an orgasm.'

Izzy was silent for just a second or two too long.

He cocked an eyebrow at her questioningly. 'You have had an orgasm, right?'

'Of course...' Majorly fiery blush this time. 'Plenty of times.'

'Izzy.' The way Zach said her name was like a parent catching a child out for lying.

'It was hard for me to get there...I always took too long to get in the mood and then Richard would pressure me and I...' Izzy gave him a helpless look '...I usually faked it.'

His frown had made a pleat between his grey eyes. 'Usually?'

'Mostly.' She bit her lip at his look. 'It was easier that way. I didn't want to hurt Richard's feelings or make him feel inadequate. Seems to me some men have such fragile egos when it comes to their sexual prowess.'

He stroked her face with his fingers. 'Being able to satisfy a partner is one of the most enjoyable aspects of sex. I want you to enjoy it, Izzy. Don't pretend with me. Be honest. Take all the time you need.'

Izzy pressed her lips against his. 'If we take too long Max might wonder what we're doing.'

He smiled against her mouth. 'I reckon he's got a pretty fair idea.' And then he kissed her.

CHAPTER ELEVEN

'THANK YOU SO much for stepping in last night,' Margie said when Izzy arrived at work the next morning. 'Doug and I had the most wonderful time. It was as if the last twenty-three years hadn't happened. We talked for hours and hours. Just as well Zach didn't get back till midnight.' Her eyes twinkled meaningfully. 'Must have been a pretty decent dinner you cooked for him. He looked very satisfied.'

Izzy had all but given up on trying to disguise her blush. Her whole body was still glowing from the passionate lovemaking she had experienced in Zach's arms last night. He had been both tender and demanding, insisting on a level of physical honesty from her that was way outside her experience. But she had loved every earth-shattering second of it.

The things she had discovered about her body had amazed her. It was capable of intense and repeated orgasms. Zach had taught her how to relax enough to embrace the powerful sensations, to let her inhibitions go, to stop over-thinking and worrying she wasn't doing things according to a schedule. He had let her choose her own timetable and his pleasure when it had come had been just as intense as hers. That the pleasure had been mutual had given their sensual encounter a depth, an almost sacred aspect she'd found strangely moving.

The only niggling worry she had was how was she going to move on after their fling was over? Falling in love with him or anyone was not part of her plan for her six months away from home. She had only just extricated herself from a long-term relationship. The last thing she wanted was to tie herself up in another one, even if Zach was the most intriguing and attractive man she had met in a long time. Strike that—had *ever* met.

'Yes, well, there's certainly nothing wrong with his appetite,' Izzy said as she popped her bag into the cupboard next to the patients' filing shelves.

'Are you going to see him again?'

'I see him practically every day.' Izzy straightened her skirt as she turned round. 'In a town this size everyone sees everyone every day.'

Margie pursed her lips in a you-can't-fool-me manner. 'You know what I mean. Are you officially a couple? I know the gossip started the moment you showed up in town but that was Charles Redbank's doing. He just wanted to make trouble. He's never forgiven Zach for booking him for speeding a couple of months back.'

'We're not officially anything.' Izzy resented even having to say that much. She wasn't used to discussing her private life with anyone other than Hannah and even then there were some things she wasn't prepared to reveal. Even to herself.

'It'd be lovely if you stayed on a bit longer,' Margie said. 'Everyone loves you. Even that old sourpuss Ida Jensen thinks you're an angel now that you've sorted out her blood-pressure medication. And Peggy McLeod's thrilled you suggested she help start up the playgroup again. She's already got a heap of toys and play equipment donated from the locals. She even got Caitlyn Graham's boyfriend, Wayne Brody, to donate some. He dropped by a bag of stuff yesterday, most of it brand new. Wasn't that nice of him?'

Izzy kept her features schooled, even though inside she was fuming. 'Unbelievably nice of him.'

Margie glanced at the diary. 'Your first patient isn't until nine-thirty. You've got time for a coffee. Want me to make you one here or shall I run up to the general store and get you a latte from Jim's new machine?'

'I'll go,' Izzy said. 'There's something I want to see Sergeant Fletcher about on the way past.'

Zach was typing up an incident report on the computer at the station when he heard the sound of footsteps coming up the path. He knew it was Izzy even before he looked up to check. His skin started to tingle; it hadn't stopped tingling since last night, but it went up a gear when he caught a whiff of summer flowers. He had gone home last night with her fragrance lingering on his skin. He had even considered skipping a shower this morning to keep it there. The way she had come apart in his arms had not only thrilled him, it had made him feel something he hadn't expected to feel.

Didn't want to feel.

He stood as she came in. 'Morning.' He knew he sounded a bit formal but he was having trouble getting that feeling he didn't want to feel back in the box where he had stashed it last night.

His manner obviously annoyed her for her brow puckered in a frown and her lips pulled tight. 'Sorry to disturb you while you're busy, but I forgot to tell you something last night.'

Would this be the bit about how she didn't want to continue their fling? He mentally prepared himself, keeping his face as blank as possible. 'Fire away.'

Her hands were balled into tight little fists by her sides, her cheeks like two bright red apples, and her toffee-brown eyes flashing. 'The toys you left for Caitlyn's kids?' She didn't give him time to say anything in response but continued; 'Wayne wouldn't let her give them to the kids.'

Zach was so relieved her tirade wasn't about ending their affair it took him a moment to respond. 'There's not much I can do about that. They were a gift and if Caitlyn didn't want to accept—'

'You're not listening to me,' she said with a little stamp of her foot. 'Caitlyn would've loved them for the kids, I know she would, she's too frightened to stand up to Wayne. But even worse than that, he passed them off as his own donation to Peggy McLeod for the community centre playgroup. He's passing off *your* gift as his own largesse. It makes my blood boil so much I want to explode!'

He came round from behind the desk and took her trembling-with-rage shoulders in his hands. 'Hey, it's not worth getting upset about it. At least the kids will have a chance to play with the toys when they go to the centre.'

Her pretty little face was scrunched up in a furious scowl. 'If that control freak lets them go. He'll probably put a stop to that too. Can't you do something? Like arrest him for making a false declaration of generosity or something?'

Zach fought back a smile as he rubbed his hands up and down her silky arms. 'My experience with guys like him is that the more you show how much they get under your skin the more they enjoy it. Best thing you can do is support Caitlyn and the kids. Helping to build up her confidence as a parent is a great start.'

She let out a sign that released her tense shoulders. 'I guess you're right...'

He tipped up her chin and meshed his gaze with her still troubled one. 'Do you have any plans for tonight?'

Her eyes lost their dullness and began to sparkle. 'I don't know. I'll have to check what Max has got planned. He might want to hang out. Watch a movie or something. He gets lonely if he's left on his own too long.'

Zach had no hope of suppressing his smile. 'Then why don't we take him on a picnic out to Blake's waterhole? I'll bring the food. I'll pick you up at six-thirty so we can catch the sunset.'

She scrunched up her face again but her eyes were dancing. 'I'm not sure Max has a pair of bathers.'

Zach gave her a glinting smile as he brought his mouth down to hers. 'Tell him he won't need them.'

Izzy spread the picnic blanket down over a patch of sunburned grass near the waterhole while Zach brought the picnic basket and their towels from the car. The sun was still high and hot enough to crisp and crackle the air with the sound of cicadas. But down by the water's edge the smell of the dusty earth was relieved by the earthy scent of cool, deep water shadowed by the overhanging craggy-armed gums. Long gold fingers of sunlight were poking between the branches to gild the water, along with a light breeze that was playfully tickling the surface.

Zach put the picnic basket down on the blanket. 'Swim first or would you like a cold drink?'

Izzy looked at him, dressed in faded blue denim jeans with their one tattered knee, his light grey body-hugging T-shirt showcasing every toned muscle of his chest and shoulders and abdomen. He looked strong and fit and capable, the sort of man you would go to in a crisis. The sort of man you could depend on, a man who was not only strong on the outside but had an inner reserve of calm deliberation. He was the sort of man who wasn't daunted by hard work or a challenging task. The way he had moved back to the bush to help his father even though it had cost him his relationship with his fiancée confirmed it. He was a man of principles, conviction. Loyalty.

It made her think of Richard, who within a couple of days of her ending their relationship had found a replacement.

Zach, on the other hand, had spent the last eighteen months quietly grieving the loss of his relationship and the future he had planned for himself, devoting his time to his father and the community. Doing whatever it took, no matter how difficult, to help his father come to terms with the limitations that had been placed on him. He didn't complain. He didn't grouse or whinge about it. He just got on with it.

Zach must have mistaken her silence for something else. 'There are no nasties in the water, if that's what's putting you off. An eel or two, a few tadpoles and frogs but nothing to be too worried about.'

A shiver of unease slithered down her spine. 'Snakes?'

'They're definitely about but more will see you than you see them.' He gave her a quick grin. 'I'll go in first and scare them away, OK?'

'Big, brave man.'

He tugged his T-shirt over his head and tossed it onto one of the sun-warmed rocks nearby. 'Yeah, well, that's more than I can say about that roommate of yours squibbing at the last minute.'

Izzy feasted her eyes on his washboard stomach and then her heart gave a little flip as he reached for the zipper on his jeans. She disguised her reaction behind humour but was sure he wasn't fooled for a second. 'It wasn't that he was scared or anything. He's got very sensitive skin. He was worried about mosquitoes. One prick and he might never recover.'

Zach's smile made her skin lift up in goose-bumps as big as the gravel they had driven over earlier. He came and stood right in front of her, dressed in nothing but his shape-hugging black underwear. He flicked the collar of her lightweight cotton blouse with two of his fingers. 'Need some help getting your gear off?'

Izzy found it hard to breathe with him so deliciously close. The smell of him, the citrus and physically active man smell of him made her insides squirm with longing. His grey-blue eyes were glinting, his mouth slanted in a sexy smile that never failed to make her feminine core contract and release in want. Her body remembered every stroke and glide and powerful thrust of his inside hers last night. Her feminine muscles tightened in feverish anticipation, the musky, silky moisture of her body automatically activated in response to his intimate proximity. 'Are you offering to do a strip search, Sergeant Fletcher?' she asked with a flirty smile.

His eyes gleamed with sensual promise as his fingers went to the buttons on her shirt. 'Let's see what you've got hidden under here, shall we?'

One by one he undid each button, somehow making it into a game of intense eroticism. His fingers scorched her skin each time he released another button from its tiny buttonhole, the action triggering yet another pulse of primal longing deep in her flesh. He peeled the shirt off her shoulders, and then tracked his finger down between her breasts, still encased in her bra. 'Beautiful.'

How one word uttered in that deep, husky tone could make her feel like a supermodel was beyond her. It wasn't just a line, a throw-away comment to get what he wanted. She knew he meant it. She could feel it in his touch, the gentle way he had of cupping her breasts once he'd released her bra, the way his thumbs stroked over her nipples with a touch that was both achingly tender and yet tantalisingly arousing.

Her cotton summer skirt was next to go, the zip going down, the little hoop of fabric circling her ankles before he took her hand and helped her step away from it like stepping out of a puddle. He put a warm, work-roughened hand to the curve of her hip just above the line of her knickers, holding her close enough to the potent heat of his body for her to feel his reaction to her closeness.

He was powerfully erect. She could feel the thrum of his blood through the lace of her knickers, the hot, urgent pressure of him stirring her senses into frantic overload.

He touched her then, a single stroke down the lace-covered seam of her body, a teasing taste of the intimate invasion to come. She whimpered as he slid her knickers aside, waiting a heart-stopping beat before he touched her again, skin on skin.

Izzy tugged his underwear down so she could do the same to him, taking him in her hands, stroking him, caressing the silky steel of him until he was breathing as raggedly as she was.

He slipped a finger inside her, swallowing her gasp as his mouth came down on hers. His kiss was passionate, thorough, and intensely erotic as his tongue tangled with hers in a cat-and-mouse caper.

Izzy's caressing of him became bolder, squeezing and releasing, smoothing up and down his length, running her fingertip over the ooze of his essence, breathing in the musky scent of mutual arousal.

There was something wildly, deeply primitive about being naked with a man in the bush. No sounds other than their hectic breathing and those of nature. The distant warble of magpies, the throaty arck-arck of a crow flying overhead, the whisper of the breeze moving through the gum leaves, sounding like thousands of finger-length strips of tinsel paper being jostled together.

Zach pressed her down on the tartan blanket, pushing the picnic things out of the way with his elbow, quickly sourcing a condom before entering her with a thrust that made her cry out with bone-deep pleasure. He set a fast rhythm that was as primal as their surroundings, the intensity of it thrilling her senses in a way she had never thought possible just a few short weeks ago. Her life in England had never felt more distant. It was like having another completely different identity that belonged back there.

Over there she was a buttoned-up girl who had spent

years of her life pretending to be happy, pleasing others rather than pleasing herself.

Out here she was a wild and wanton woman, having smoking-hot sex with a man she hadn't known a fortnight ago.

And now...now she was rocking in his arms as if her world began and ended with him. The physicality of their relationship was shocking, the blunt, almost brutal honesty of the needs of their bodies as they strove for completion was as carnal as two wild animals mating. Even the sound of her cries as she came were those of a woman she didn't know, had never encountered before. Wild, shrieking cries that spoke of a depth of passion that had never been tapped into or expressed before.

Zach's release was not as vocal but Izzy felt the power of it as he tensed, pumped and then flowed.

He didn't move for a long moment. His body rested on hers in the aftermath, his breathing slowly returning to normal as she stroked her hands up and down his back and shoulders, their bodies still intimately joined.

'I think there's a pebble sticking into my butt,' Izzy finally said.

He rolled her over so she was lying on top of him, his eyes heavily lidded, sleepy with satiation. 'Better?'

'Much.'

He circled her right breast with a lazy finger. 'Ever skinny dipped before?'

'Not with a man present.' Izzy gave him a wry smile. 'I did it with Hannah and a couple of other girlfriends when we were thirteen at my birthday party. It was a dare.'

His finger made a slow, nerve-tingling circuit of her

other breast. 'Is that how the crazy birthday stuff with her started?'

Izzy sent her own fingers on an exploration of his flat brown nipple nestled amongst his springy chest hair. 'Come to think of it, yes. She was always on about me being too worried about what other people thought. She made it her mission in life to shock me out of my "aristocratic mediocrity", as she calls it.'

He stroked his hand over the flank of her thigh. 'Somehow mediocre isn't the first word that comes to mind when I think of you.'

Izzy angled her head at him. 'So what word does?'

He gave her a slow smile that crinkled up the corners of his eyes in a devastatingly attractive manner. 'Cute. Funny. Sexy.'

She traced the outline of his smile with her fingertip. 'I never felt sexy before. Not the way I do with you.' She bit down on her lip, wondering if she'd been too honest, revealed too much.

He brushed her lower lip with his thumb. 'You do that a lot.'

'What?'

'Bite your lip.'

Izzy had to stop her teeth from doing it again. 'It's a nervous habit. Half the time I'm not even aware I'm doing it.'

His thumb caressed her lip as if soothing it from the assault of her teeth. 'Why don't you come down here and bite mine instead?'

Izzy leaned down and started nibbling at his lower lip, using her teeth to tug and tease. She used her tongue to sweep over where her teeth had been, before starting the process all over again. Nip. Tug. Nip. Tug.

He gave little grunts of approval, one of his hands splayed in her hair as he held her head close to his. 'Harder,' he commanded.

A shudder of pleasure shimmied down her spine as his hand fisted in her hair. She pulled at his lip with her teeth, stroked it with her tongue and then pushed her tongue into his mouth to meet his. Zach murmured his pleasure and took control of the kiss, his masterful tongue darting and diving around hers.

It was an exhilarating kiss, wild and abandoned and yet still with an element of tenderness that ambushed her emotionally.

She wasn't supposed to be feeling anything but lust for this man.

This was a fling.

A casual hook-up like all her girlfriends experienced from time to time. It was a chance to own her sexuality, to express it without the confining and formal bounds of a relationship.

She was only here for another couple of weeks. She was moving on to new sights and experiences, filling her six months away from home with adventure and memories to look back on in the years to come.

Falling in love would be a crazy…a totally disastrous thing to do…

Izzy eased off Zach while he dealt with the condom. She gathered her tousled hair and tied it into a makeshift knot, using the tresses as an anchor. Her body tingled with the memory of his touch as she got to her feet, tiny aftershocks of pleasure rippling through her.

She was dazed by sensational sex, that's all it was.

It wasn't love. How could it be?

Maybe it was time to cool off.

'Are you sure it's safe to swim here?'

'Not for diving but it's fine for a dip.' He took her hand and led her down to the water. 'Not quite St Barts, is it?'

Izzy glanced at him. 'You've been there?'

'Once.' He looked out over the water as if he was seeing the exclusive Caribbean holiday destination in his mind's eye, his mouth curled up in a cynical arc. 'With my mother and her new family when I was fourteen. Cost her husband a packet. I'm sure he only took us all there to make a point of how good her life was with him instead of my father. I didn't go on holidays with them after that. I got tired of having all that wealth thrust in my face.'

Izzy moved her fingers against his. 'I hated most of my family holidays. I'm sure we only went to most of the places we went to because that's where my parents thought people expected to see us. Skiing at exclusive lodges in Aspen. Sailing around the Mediterranean on yachts that cost more than most people ever see in a lifetime. I would've loved to go camping under the stars in the wilderness but, no, it was butlers and chauffeurs and five stars all the way.'

He looked at her with a wry smile tilting his mouth. 'Funny, isn't it, that you always want what you don't have?'

I have what I want right now. Izzy quickly filed away the thought. She looked down at the mud that was squelching between her toes. The water was refreshingly cool against her heated skin. She went in a little further, holding Zach's hand for balance until she was waist deep. 'Mmm, that's lovely.' She went in a bit deeper but something cold and slimy brushed against her leg and she yelped and sprang back and clung to Zach like a limpet. 'Eeek! What was that?'

He held her against him, laughing softly. 'It was just a bit of weed. Nothing to worry about. You're safe with me.'

Her arms were locked around his neck, her legs wrapped around his waist and her mouth within touching distance of his. She watched as his gaze went to her mouth, the way his lashes lowered in that sleepily hooded way a man did when he was thinking about sex. A new wave of desire rolled through her as his mouth came down and fused with hers.

You're safe with me.

Izzy wasn't safe. Not the way she wanted to be. Not the way she needed to be.

She was in very great danger indeed.

CHAPTER TWELVE

As ZACH PACKED the picnic things back in the car Izzy looked up at the brilliant night sky with its scattering of stars like handfuls of diamonds flung across a bolt of dark blue velvet. The air was still warm and the night orchestra's chorus had recruited two extra voices: a tawny frogmouth owl and a vixen fox, looking for a mate.

That distinctive bark was a sound from home, making Izzy feel a sudden pang of homesickness. She wondered if sounds like those of a lonely feral fox had caused Zach's mother to grieve for the life she had left behind. Had the years fighting drought and dust and flies or floods and failed crops and flyblown sheep finally broken her spirit? Or had she simply fallen out of love with her husband? Leaving a husband one no longer loved was understandable, but leaving a child to travel to the other side of the world was something else again. Leaving Zach behind must have been a very difficult decision.

Izzy couldn't imagine a mother choosing her freedom over her child, but she recognised that not all mothers found the experience as satisfying and fulfilling as others.

Leaving Zach behind...

The words reverberated inside her head. That was what she would have to do in a matter of a fortnight. She would never see him again. He would move on with his life, no doubt in a year or two find a good, sensible, no-nonsense country girl to settle down with, raise a family and work the land as his father and grandfather and forebears had done before him. She imagined him sitting at the scrubbed pine kitchen table at Fletcher Downs homestead surrounded by his wife and children. He would make a wonderful father. She had seen him with Caitlyn's children, generous, gentle and calm.

Izzy heard his footfall on the gravel as he came to join her. 'Have you found the Southern Cross?' he asked.

'I think so.' She pointed to a constellation of stars in the south. 'Is that it there?'

He followed the line of her arm and nodded. 'Yep, that's it. Good work. You must've done your research.'

Izzy turned and looked at him, something in her heart contracting as if a hand had grabbed at it and squeezed. 'Would you ever consider living somewhere else?' she asked.

A frown flickered over his brow. 'You mean like back in the city?'

Izzy wasn't sure what she meant. She wasn't sure why she had even asked. 'Will you quit your work as a cop and take over Fletcher Downs once your father officially retires?'

He looked back at the dark overturned bowl of the sky, his gaze going all the way to the horizon, where a thin lip of light lingered just before the sun dipped to wake the other side of the world. 'I love my work as a cop…well, most of the time. But the land is in my blood. The Fletcher name goes back a long way in these parts, all the way back to the first European settlers. I'm my dad's only heir. I can't afford to pay a manager for ever. The property would have to be sold if I didn't take it on full time.'

'But is that what *you* want?'

He continued to focus on the distant horizon with a grim set to his features. 'What I want is my dad to get back to full health and mobility but that doesn't look like it's going to happen any time soon.'

'But at least he's becoming more socially active,' Izzy said. 'That's a great step forward. Margie's determined to get him out more. It would be so nice if they got together, don't you think?'

He looked back at her with that same grave look. 'My father will never get married again. He's been burned once. He would never go back for a second dose.'

'But that's crazy,' Izzy said. 'Margie loves him. She's loved him since she was a girl. They belong together. Anyone can see that.'

His lip curled upwards but it wasn't so much mocking as wry. 'Stick to your medical journals, Izzy. Those romance novels you read are messing with your head.'

It's not my head they're messing with, Izzy thought as she followed him back to the car.

It was her heart.

Zach brought a beer out to his father on the veranda a couple of days later. 'Here you go. But only the one. Remember what the doctor said about drinking plenty of clear fluids.'

'Thanks.' Doug took a long sip, and then let a silence slip past before asking, 'You seeing her tonight?'

Zach reached down to tickle Popeye's ears. 'Not tonight.'

'Wise of you.'

'What's that supposed to mean?'

Doug took another sip of his beer before answering. 'Better not get too used to having her around. She's going to be packing up and leaving before you know it.'

Zach tried to ignore the savage twist of his insides at the thought of Izzy driving out of town once her locum was up. He'd heard a whisper the locals were going to use the Shearers' Ball as a send-off for her. William Sawyer and his wife would be back from their trip soon and life would return to normal in Jerringa Ridge.

Normal.

What a weird word to describe his life. When had it ever been normal? Growing up since the age of ten without a mother. Years of putting up with his father's ongoing bitterness over his marriage break-up. For years he hadn't even been able to mention his mother without his father flinching as if he had landed a punch on him.

Dealing with the conflicted emotions of visiting his mother in her gracious home in Surrey, where he didn't fit in with the formal furniture or her even more formal ridiculously wealthy new husband who never seemed to wear anything but a suit and a silk cravat, even on St Barts. Those gut-wrenching where-do-I-belong feelings intensifying once her new sons Jules and Oliver had been born. Coming back home and feeling just as conflicted trying to settle back in to life at Fletcher Downs or at boarding school.

Always feeling the outsider.

'I know what I'm doing, Dad.'

His father glanced at him briefly before turning to look at the light fading over the paddocks. It was a full minute, maybe longer before he spoke. 'I'm not going to get any better than this, am I? No point pretending I am.'

Zach found the sudden shift in conversation disorienting. 'Sure you are. You're doing fine.' He was doing it again. It was his fall-back position. A pattern of the last twenty-three years he couldn't seem to get out of—playing Pollyanna to his father's woe-is-me moods. He could recall all the pep-talk phrases he'd used in the past: *Time heals everything. You'll find someone else. Take it one day at a time. Baby steps. Everything happens for a reason.*

Doug's hand tightened on his can of beer until the aluminium crackled. 'I should've married Margie. I should've done it years ago. Now it's too late.'

It's never too late was on the tip of Zach's tongue but he refrained from voicing it. 'Is that what Margie wants? Marriage?'

'It's what most women want, isn't it?' His father gave his beer can another crunch. 'A husband, a family, a home they can be proud of. Security.'

'Margie's already got a family and a house and her job is secure,' Zach said. 'Seems to me what she wants is companionship.'

His father's top lip curled in a manner so like his own it was disquieting to witness. 'And what sort of companion am I? I can't even get on a stepladder and change a bloody light bulb.'

'There's more to a relationship than who puts out the garbage or takes the dog for a walk,' Zach said.

His father didn't seem to be listening. He was still looking out over the paddocks with a frown between his eyes. 'I didn't see it at the time...all those years ago I didn't see Margie for who she was. She was always just one of the local girls, fun to be around but didn't stand out. Then I met your mother.' He made a self-deprecating sound. 'What a fool I was to think I could make someone like her happy. I tried for ten years to keep her. Ten years of living with the dread she would one day pack up and leave. And then she did.' He clicked his fingers. *Snap.* 'She was gone.'

Zach remembered it all too well. He could still remember exactly where he had been standing on the veranda as he'd watched his mother drive away. He had gripped the veranda rail so tightly his hands had ached for days. He had watched with his heart feeling as heavy as a headstone in his chest. His mouth had been as dry as the red dust his mother's car had stirred up as she'd wheeled away.

For weeks, months, even years every time he heard a car come up the long driveway he would feel his heart leap in hope that she was coming back.

She never did.

Doug looked at Zach. 'It wasn't her fault. Not all of it. I was fighting to keep this place going after your grandfather died and then your grandmother so soon after. I didn't give her the attention she needed. You can't take an orchid out of an English conservatory and expect it to survive in the Outback. You have to nurture it, protect it.'

'Do you still love her?'

Doug's mouth twisted. 'There's a part of me that will always love your mother. Maybe not the same way

I did. It's like keeping that old pair of work boots near the back door. I'm not quite ready to part with them yet.'

'I'm not sure Mum would appreciate being compared to a pair of your old smelly work boots,' Zach said wryly, thinking of his mother's penchant for cashmere and pearls and designer shoes.

A small sad smile skirted around the edges of Doug's mouth. 'No…probably not.'

A silence passed.

'Why's it too late for you and Margie?' Zach asked. 'You're only fifty-eight. She's, what? Fifty-two or -three? You could have a good thirty or forty years together.'

'Look at me, Zach.' His father's eyes glittered with tightly held-back emotion. 'Take a good look. I'm like this now, shuffling about like a man in his eighties. What am I going to be like in five or even ten years' time? You heard what the specialist said. I was lucky to get this far. I can't do it to Margie. I can't turn her into a carer instead of a wife and lover. It'd make her hate me.' His chin quivered as he fought to keep his voice under control. 'I couldn't bear to have another woman I love end up hating me.'

'I think you're underestimating Margie,' Zach said. 'She's not like Mum. She's strong and dependable and loyal.'

'And you're such a big expert on women, aren't you, Zach? You've got one broken engagement on the leader board already. How soon before there's another?'

'There's not going to be another.'

'Why?' His father's lip was still up in that nasty little curl. 'Because you won't risk asking her, will you?'

Zach could barely get the words out through his clenched teeth. 'Ask who?'

His father pushed himself to his feet, nailing Zach with his gaze. 'That toffee-nosed little doctor you spend every spare moment of your time with.'

'I'm not in love with Isabella Courtney.'

'No, of course you're not.' Doug gave a scornful grunt of laughter. 'Keep on telling yourself that, son. If nothing else, it'll make the day she leaves a little easier on you.'

Izzy knew it was cowardly of her to pretend to be busy with catching up on emails and work-related stuff two nights in a row but spending all her spare time with Zach was making it increasingly difficult for her to keep her emotions separate from the physical side of their relationship. No wonder sex was called making love. Every look, every touch, every kiss, every spine-tingling orgasm seemed to up the ante until she wasn't sure what she felt any more. Was it love or was it lust?

Had it been a mistake to indulge in an affair with him? She had spent four years making love—*having sex*—with Richard and had never felt anything like the depth of feeling she did with Zach, and she had only known him three weeks.

And there was only one to go.

Margie looked very downcast when Izzy got to the clinic the next morning. She was sitting behind the reception desk with red-rimmed eyes and her shoulders slumped. 'Don't ask.'

'Doug?'

Margie reached for a tissue from the box on her desk. 'He said it's best if we don't see each other any more, only as friends. I've been friends with him for most of my life but it's not enough. I want more.'

'Oh, Margie, I'm so sorry. I thought things were going so well.'

Margie dabbed at her eyes. 'It's my fault for thinking I could change his mind. I should have left well alone. Now he knows how I feel about him it makes me feel so stupid. Like a lovesick schoolgirl or something.'

'Is there anything I can do?'

'Not unless you can make him fall out of love with his ex-wife.'

Izzy frowned. 'Do you really think that's what it's about?'

'What else could it be? Olivia was his grand passion.' Margie plucked another tissue out of the box and blew her nose.

'What if it's more to do with his limitations? He's a proud man. Having to rely on others for help must be really tough on someone like him.'

'But I love him. I don't care if he can't get around the way he used to. Why can't he just accept that I love him no matter what?'

Izzy gave her a sympathetic look. 'Maybe he needs more time. From what I've read of his notes, his injuries were pretty severe. And this latest bout of renal colic has probably freaked him out a bit. It's very common for every ache or pain in someone who's suffered a major illness or trauma to get magnified in their head.'

Margie gave a sound of agreement. 'Well, enough about me and my troubles. How are you and Zach getting on?'

'Fine.'

'Just fine?'

Izzy picked off a yellowed leaf from the pot plant on

the counter. 'There's nothing serious going on between us. We both know and understand that.'

'Would you like it to be more?'

'I'm leaving at the end of next week.'

'That's not the answer I was looking for,' Margie said.

'It's the only one I'm prepared to give.'

Margie looked at her thoughtfully for a lengthy moment. 'Don't make the same mistake I made, Izzy. I should've told Doug years ago what I felt for him. Now it's too late.'

'I spent four years with a man and then realised I didn't love him enough to marry him,' Izzy said. 'What makes you think I would be so confident about my feelings after less than four weeks?'

Margie gave her a sage look. 'Because when you know you just know.'

CHAPTER THIRTEEN

Izzy WALKED DOWN to the community centre during her lunch break. She had arranged to meet Peggy McLeod there as well as Caitlyn Graham, who had finally agreed to work with Peggy in a mentor and mentee role. Peggy as a mother and grandmother with years of wisdom and experience working in the community was just what Caitlyn needed as a role model. Peggy had even offered to babysit Skylar occasionally when the boys were at school so Caitlyn could get a bit of a break. But when Izzy arrived at the centre Peggy was on her own.

'Where's Caitlyn?'

Peggy gave Izzy a miffed look over her shoulder as she placed a box of building blocks on the shelves one of the local farmers had made specially. 'Decided she had better things to do.'

'But I confirmed it with her yesterday,' Izzy said. 'She said she was looking forward to it. It was the first time I'd ever seen her excited about something.'

'Yes, well, she called me not five minutes ago and told me she's changed her mind.'

Changed her mind or had it changed for her? Izzy wondered. 'I think I'd better go and check on her. Maybe one of the kids is sick or something.'

'The boys are at school,' Peggy said. 'I waved to them in the playground when I drove past.'

'Maybe Skylar's sick.'

'Then why didn't she just say so?'

Izzy frowned. 'What *did* she say?'

Peggy pursed her lips. 'Just that she'd changed her mind. Told me she didn't want me babysitting for her either. I've brought up five kids and I'm a grandmother twelve times over. What does she think I am? An axe murderer or something?'

'Don't take it personally,' Izzy said. 'She's not used to having anyone step in and help her. I'll duck out there now and see if I can get her to change her mind.'

Izzy thought about calling Zach to come with her but changed her mind at the last minute. His car wasn't at the station in any case and she didn't want to make a big issue out of what could just be a case of Caitlyn's lack of self-esteem kicking in. She'd tried calling her a couple of times but the phone had gone to message bank.

Caitlyn's old car was parked near the house but apart from the frenzied barking of the dog near the tank stand there was no sign of life. Izzy walked tentatively to the front door, saying, 'Nice doggy, good doggy,' with as much sincerity as she could muster. She put her hand up to knock but the door suddenly opened and she found herself face to face with a thick-set man in his late twenties, who was even scarier than the dog lunging on its chain to her left.

'What do you want?' the man snarled.

'Um… Hello, is Caitlyn home? I'm Isabella Courtney, the locum filling in for—'

'Did she call you?'

'No, I just thought I'd drop past and—'

'She don't need no doctor so you can get back in your fancy car and get the hell out of here.'

The sound of Skylar crying piteously in one of the back rooms of the house made Izzy's heart lurch. 'Is Skylar OK? She sounds terribly upset. Is she—?'

'You want me to let the dog off?' His cold eyes glared at her through the tattered mesh of the screen door.

Izzy garnered what was left of her courage. She straightened her shoulders and looked him in the eye with what she hoped looked like steely determination. 'I'd like to talk to Caitlyn before I leave.'

Wayne suddenly shoved the screen door wide open, which forced her to take a couple of rapid steps backwards that sent her backwards off the veranda to land in an ungainly heap on her bottom in the dust. 'I said clear off,' he said.

Izzy scrambled to her feet, feeling a fool and a coward and so angry and utterly powerless she wanted to scream. But she knew the best thing to do was to leave and call Zach as soon as she was out of danger. She dusted off the back of her skirt and walked back to her car with as much dignity as she could muster. Her hand trembled uncontrollably as she tried to get her car key in the ignition slot to start the engine. It took her five tries to do it. Her heart was hammering in her chest and terrified sobs were choking out of her throat as she drove out of the driveway.

Zach was on the road when he got a distressed call from Izzy. 'Hey, slow down, sweetheart. I can't understand a word you're saying.'

She was crying and gasping, her breathing so erratic

it sounded like she was choking. 'I think Wayne's hurt Caitlyn. She didn't turn up at the playgroup. I heard Skylar screaming in the background. I think he'd been drinking. I could smell it. You have to do something. You have to hurry.'

'Where are you?'

'I—I'm on the road just past the t-turnoff.'

'Stop driving. Pull over. Do it right now.' He didn't let out his breath until he heard her do as he'd commanded. 'Good girl. Now wait for me. I'm only a few minutes away. I'll call Rob for back-up. Just stay put, OK?'

'OK…'

Zach called his colleague and quickly filled him in. He drove as fast as he could to where Izzy was parked on the side of the road. She was as white as a stick of chalk and tumbled out of the car even before he had pulled to a halt.

He gathered her close, reassuring himself she was all right before he put her from him. 'I'm going to check things out. I've called the volunteer ambulance and put them on standby. I want you to stay here until I see what the go is. I'll call you if we need you. It might not be as serious as you think.'

Her eyes looked as big as a Shetland pony's. 'You won't get hurt, will you?'

'Course not.' He quickly kissed her on the forehead. 'I've got a gun, remember?'

Izzy took a steadying breath as she waited for Zach to contact her. It seemed like ten hours but it was only ten minutes before he called her to inform her Caitlyn and Skylar were fine. 'Brody was his usual charming self,' he said. 'But Caitlyn insisted he hadn't hurt her or the child. She didn't appear to have any marks or bruises and the child seemed settled enough. She was sound asleep when I looked in on her. Apparently Brody was insisting she take a nap and wouldn't let Caitlyn go in to comfort her.'

'And you believed him?'

'I can't arrest him without evidence and Caitlyn swears he didn't do anything.'

Izzy blew out a breath of frustration. 'If he didn't hurt her today he will do sooner or later. I just know it.'

'Welcome to the world of tricky relationships.'

They can't get any trickier than the one I'm in, Izzy thought. 'Can I see you after work?'

'Not too busy with emails and video calls to your friends?'

'Not tonight.'

'Good,' he said. 'I happen to be free too.'

Izzy got back to the clinic in time to see her list of afternoon patients but just as she was about to finish for the day Margie popped her head into her consulting room. 'You got a minute?'

'Sure.' Izzy put down the pen she had been using to write up her last patient's details, mentally preparing herself for another emotional outpouring of Margie's unrequited love story. It wasn't that she didn't want to listen or support her. It was just too close to what she was feeling about Zach. How could it be possible to fall in love with someone so quickly? Did that sort of thing really happen or was that just in Hollywood movies? Was she imagining how she felt? Was it just this crazy lust fest she had going on with him that was colouring her judgement?

Margie rolled her lips together, looking awkward and embarrassed as she came into the room. 'It's not about Doug or anything like that… It's a personal thing. A health thing.'

'What's the problem?'

'I found a lump.'

'In your breast?'

Margie nodded, and then gave her lower lip a little chew. 'I've been a bit slack about doing my own checks but when you ordered that mammogram for Kathleen Fisher earlier today it got me thinking. I went to the bathroom just then. I found a lump.'

Izzy got up from her chair and came from behind the desk. 'Hop on the examination table and I'll have a feel of it for you. Try not to worry too much. Breast tissue can go through lots of changes for any number of reasons.'

Margie lay back on the table and unbuttoned her blouse and unclipped her bra. 'I can't believe I've been so stupid not to check my own breasts. I haven't done it for months, maybe even a couple of years.'

Izzy palpated Margie's left breast where, high in the upper part, there was a definite firm nodule, about the size of a walnut. 'You're right, there is a lump there. Is it tender at all?'

'No, it's not sore at all. It's cancer, isn't it?'

'Hang on, Margie. It could be any of several things. It could be a cyst, some hormonal thickening, maybe a benign tumour. It could possibly be cancer, but we have to do some tests in Bourke to tell what it is.'

'What do we do now?' Margie's expression was stricken. 'I'm worried. What am I going to tell the kids?'

'We'll do what we always do—we'll go step by step, figure out what the lump is and then fix it,' Izzy said. 'First we get a mammogram and ultrasound. Then, at the same time, we'll get the mammogram people to take a needle sample of the lump. That should give us the diagnosis. If it's a cyst, we just aspirate the fluid with a needle and that's usually the end of it. If the biopsy shows cancer cells, we get a surgeon to deal with it.'

'If it's cancer, will I have to have a mastectomy?'

'Mastectomies are very uncommon these days. Usually just the lump plus one lymph gland is removed, and then the breast gets some radiotherapy. If the lymph node was positive, possibly some more surgery to the armpit and maybe some chemo or hormonal therapies.'

Margie swung her legs off the examination table, her expression contorted with anguish as her fingers fumbled with the buttons on her blouse. 'I don't want to die. I have so much I want to do. I want to see my grandkids grow up. I want Doug to—' She suddenly looked at Izzy. 'Oh, God, what am I going to say to Doug? He'll never want me now, not if I've got cancer.'

Izzy took Margie's hand and gave it a comforting squeeze. 'No one's talking about dying. These days breast cancer is a very treatable disease when it's caught early. Let's take this one step at a time.'

'But who will run the clinic while I go to Bourke for the biopsy?'

'I'm sure I'll manage for a day without you,' Izzy said. 'I can divert the phone to mine, or maybe I could ask Peggy to sit by the phone. I'm sure she wouldn't mind.'

Margie sank her teeth into her lip. 'You know…the scary thing is if you hadn't been here filling in for William Sawyer I might not have bothered asking him to check me. I've known him so long it's kind of embarrassing, you know?'

'A lot of women feel the same way you do about seeing a male doctor for anything gynaecological or for breast issues, but all doctors, male or female, are trained to assess both male and female conditions.' Izzy wrote out the biopsy order form and a referral letter. 'I'll phone the surgeon and see if I can get you in this week. The sooner we know what we're dealing with the better.'

'Thanks, Izzy.' Margie clutched the letter to her chest. 'I don't mind if you tell Zach about this. I think Doug would want to know.'

'Why don't you call Doug yourself?'

Margie's eyes watered up. 'Because I'll just howl and blubber like a baby. I think it's better if he hears it from Zach. Will you be seeing him tonight?'

'He's dropping in after work.'

Margie's hand stalled on the doorknob as she looked back at Izzy over her shoulder. 'William is going to retire in a year or so. Maybe if you stayed you could job-share or something.'

'I can't stay. My home is in England.' She said it like a mantra. Like a creed. 'It's where I belong.'

'Is that where your heart is?'

'Of course.' Izzy kept her expression under such tight control it was painful. 'Where else would it be?'

Izzy opened the door to Zach a couple of hours later. 'Hi.'

He ran a finger down the length of her cheek in a touch as light as a brushstroke. 'You OK?'

She blew out a long exhausted-sounding breath. 'What a day.'

He closed the door behind him and reached for her, cupping her face in his hands and kissing her gently on the mouth. A soft, comforting kiss that was somehow far more meaningful and moving than if he'd let loose with a storm of passion. It was his sensitivity that made her heart contract. It wasn't because she was in love with him. That thought was off limits. Her brain was barricaded like a crime scene. Cordoned off. *Do Not Enter.*

He pulled back to look at her, still holding her hands in his. 'I've got some good news.'

Izzy gave him a weary look. 'I could certainly do with some. What is it?'

'Caitlyn Graham filed a domestic assault complaint an hour ago. That's why I'm late. Rob's taking Wayne Brody to Bourke to formally charge him.'

Izzy clutched at his hands. 'Is she all right? Should I go and see her?'

'She's gone to Peggy McLeod's place with the kids. I thought you'd had enough drama for one day.'

'What happened? I thought you were certain he hadn't hurt her when you went out there?'

'He hadn't at that stage,' Zach said. 'He'd verbally threatened her. Refused to let her leave the house, that sort of thing. But a couple of hours after we left, when the boys got home from school on the bus he started trying to lay into her. Apparently he's done it before but never in front of the boys. Jobe called triple zero.'

'Are you sure Caitlyn's not hurt? Are the kids OK?'

'Brody was too tanked to do much after the first swing, which Caitlyn luckily managed to dodge. She barricaded herself and the kids in the bathroom and waited for Rob and me to arrive.'

Izzy shuddered at the thought of the terror Caitlyn and the kids must have felt. 'I'm so glad she's finally out of danger. I felt sure it would only be a matter of time before he did something to her or one of the kids. He was so threatening to me. I thought he was going to assault me for sure.'

'If he had, he would've had me to answer to.' A quiver went through her at the implacability in his tone and his grey-blue eyes had a hard, self-satisfied glitter to them as he added, 'As it was, I already had a little score to settle with him.'

Izzy ran a gentle fingertip over the angry graze marks on the backs of the knuckles on his right hand. 'You wouldn't do anything outside the law, would you, Sergeant?' she asked.

He gave her an inscrutable smile. 'I'm one of the good guys, remember?'

She stepped up on tiptoe and pressed a kiss to his lips. 'I didn't realise they still made men like you any more.'

He threaded his fingers through her hair, gently massaging her scalp. 'You sure you're OK?'

Sensitive. Thoughtful. Gallant. What's not to love?

Izzy stepped back behind the yellow and black tape in her head. 'Margie has a lump in her breast.'

His brows snapped together in shock. 'Cancer?'

'I don't know yet. She has to have a mammogram and ultrasound and possibly a fine needle biopsy. I've managed to get her an appointment the day after tomorrow.' Izzy let out a breath. 'She wanted me to tell you so you could tell your dad.'

'Why doesn't she want to tell him herself?'

'I asked her the same thing but she's worried about getting too upset.'

He dropped his hands from her head and raked one through his own hair. 'Poor Margie. This town would be lost without her. My dad would be lost without her.'

'What a pity he hasn't told her that,' Izzy said on another sigh.

He gave her a thoughtful look. 'He will when he realises it.'

CHAPTER FOURTEEN

'CANCER?' DOUG'S FACE blanched. 'Why on earth didn't she tell me herself?'

Zach mentally rolled his eyes. 'You're the one who blew her off because she was getting too close.'

His father looked the colour of grey chalk. 'Is it serious? Is she going to die?'

'I don't know the answer to that. No one does yet. Izzy's organised a biopsy for her in Bourke. We'll know more after the results of that come through.'

'I need to see her. Will you drive me there now? I just want to see her to make sure she's all right.'

'What, *now?*'

'Why not now?' Doug said. 'She shouldn't be on her own at a time like this. Better still, I'll pack a bag and stay with her. I'll go with her to the appointment. She'll want someone with her. Might as well be me.'

Zach felt a warm spill of hope spread through his chest. 'You sure about this? You haven't stayed anywhere overnight other than hospital or rehab since the accident.'

Doug gave him a glowering look. 'I'm not a complete invalid, you know. I might not be able to do some of the things I used to do but I can still support a friend when they need me. Margie was the first person other than you to come to see me after the accident. She sat for days by my bedside. It's only right that I support her through this.'

Three days later Izzy opened the letter from the surgeon with trembling hands. Margie and Doug were sitting together in her consulting room, holding hands like teenagers on their first date.

'I want you to know I'm going to marry Margie, no matter what that letter says,' Doug said. 'I've already talked to Reverend Taylor.'

Izzy acknowledged that with a smile. Zach had already told her the good news. Now it was time for the bad news. She looked at the typed words on the single sheet of paper with the pathology report attached. She breathed out a sigh of relief. Not such bad news after all. 'It's not as bad as it could be. It's a DCIS—'

'What's that?' Doug asked, before Izzy could explain.

'DCIS is duct cancer in situ. It's not cancer but a step before you to get to cancer. It's like catching the horse just before it bolts.'

'So I don't have cancer? But you said duct cancer. I don't understand. Do I have it or not?' Margie asked.

'I'll try and explain it the best I can,' Izzy said. 'Think of it like this. Our body is made up of trillions of cells. Each cell has a computer program in it, telling it what to do. The computer program becomes damaged in some cell and the cell doesn't do what it's supposed to do. The worst-case scenario is when a whole lot of damage occurs, the cell goes out of control, starts multiplying too many copies of itself and won't stop. The copies spread throughout the body. That's cancer. But DCIS is where only a little bit of damage has occurred so far—the cell is a bit iffy when it comes to taking orders, but isn't yet out of control. If the lump is fully removed the problem has been cured.'

'Cured? Just by removing the lump? You mean surgery will fix this?' Doug asked.

'Yes, but the surgeon is still recommending radiotherapy afterwards because although the palpable lump of DCIS will be removed, there could be other unstable cells in the breast about to do the same thing. You'll need regular follow-up but it's certainly a lot better news than it could have been.'

Doug hugged Margie so tightly it looked like he was going to snap her in two. 'I can't believe what a fool I've been for all these years. We'll get married as soon as it can be arranged and go on a fancy cruise for our honeymoon once you've got the all-clear.'

Margie laughed and hugged him back. 'I feel like I've won the lottery. I'm not going to die and I've got the man of my dreams wanting to marry me.' She turned to Izzy. 'How can I thank you?'

'Nothing to thank me for,' Izzy said. 'I'm just doing my job.'

Which will end in two days' time.

Zach had been dreading the Shearers' Ball. Not just because too many of the locals had too much to drink and he had to be the fun police, but because it was the last night Izzy was going to be in town. Neither of them had mentioned that fact over the last couple of days. The drama with Margie and then the relief of his father finally getting his act together had pushed the elephant out of the room.

Now it was back…but Zach was painfully aware its bags were packed.

As soon as Zach arrived at the community centre where the country-style ball was being held he saw Izzy. She was wearing a fifties-style dress with a circle skirt in a bright shade of red that made her look like a poppy in a field of dandelions. He had never seen her look more beautiful. He had never seen *anyone* look more beautiful. Her hair was up in that half casual, half formal style, her creamy skin was highlighted with the lightest touch of make-up and those gorgeous kissable lips shimmered with lip-gloss.

The locals surrounded her, each one wanting to have their share of her. Caitlyn Graham was there with the kids, looking relaxed and happy for the first time in years. Peggy McLeod was cuddling Skylar and smiling at something Caitlyn had said to Izzy.

Jim Collis wandered over with a beer in his hand. 'She's something else, isn't she?'

Zach kept his expression masked. 'I see you got your tyres fixed.'

'Cost me a fortune.' Jim took another swig of his beer. 'Hey, good news about Margie and your old man. About bloody time. Look at them over there. Anyone would think they were sixteen again.'

Zach looked towards the back of the community hall where his father was seated next to Margie on a hay bale, their hands joined, his father's walking frame proving a rather useful receptacle for Margie's handbag as well as a place to put their drinks and a plate of the delicious food Peggy and her team had organised. 'Yeah. I'm happy for him. For both of them.'

'So…' Jim gave Zach a nudge with his elbow. 'What about you and the doc?'

'She's leaving tomorrow.' Zach said it as if the words weren't gnawing a giant hole in his chest. 'Got a new locum position in Brisbane. Starting on Monday.'

'Brisbane's not so far away. Maybe you could—'

'What would be the point?' Zach said. 'She's going back to England in July. It's where she belongs. Excuse me.' He gave Jim a dismissive look. 'I'm going to get something to drink.'

Izzy saw Zach standing to the left of the entrance of the community centre with a can of lemonade in his hand. He had his cop face on, acknowledging the locals who greeted him with a stiff movement of his lips as if it physically pained him to crack a full smile. She knew events like these were often quite stressful for country police officers. There were always a couple of locals who liked to drink a little too much and things could turn from a fun-loving party into an out of control mêlée in less time than it took to shake a cocktail. Friends could become enemies in a matter of minutes and the cop on duty had to be ready to control things and keep order.

Izzy had spent a few hours last night with Zach but the topic of her leaving had been carefully skirted around. She'd told him she was looking forward to the Brisbane locum but even as she'd said the words she'd felt a sinkhole of sadness open up inside her. It was like her mouth was saying one thing while her heart was saying another. *Feeling* another. But it wasn't like she could tell him how she felt. What woman in her right mind would tell a man she had only known a month that she loved him? He'd think she was mad.

It was a fling. A casual hook-up that had suited both of them. They had both needed to get over their broken engagements. Their short-term relationship had been a healing process, an exercise in closure so now they were both free to move on with their lives.

The trouble was it didn't feel like a fling. It had never felt like a fling.

Izzy went over to him with a plate of savoury nibbles Peggy had thrust in her hand on her way past. 'Having fun over here all by yourself?'

He gave her a dry look. 'You know that word "wall-flower"? I'm more of a wall tree.'

She smiled. 'I'm pretty good on a city nightclub dance floor but out here among the hay bales I'm not sure what might happen.'

'Are you asking me to dance with you?'

Izzy was asking much more than that and wondered if he could see it in her eyes. His expression, however, was much harder to read. He had that invisible wall around him but whether it was because he was on duty or because he was holding back from her for other reasons she couldn't quite tell. 'Not if you don't want to.'

He put his can of lemonade on a nearby trestle table. 'Come on.' He took her hand as the music started. 'One dance then I'm back on duty.'

As soon as his arms went around her Izzy felt as if everyone else in the community centre had faded into the background. It was just Zach and her on the hay-strewn dance floor, their bodies moving as one in a waltz to a poignant country music ballad.

Zach's breath stirred her hair as he turned her round in a manoeuvre that would have got a ten out of ten on a reality dance show. 'You know what happens if you play country music backwards?'

Izzy looked up at him with a quizzical smile. 'No, what?'

'You get your job back, your dead dog comes back to life and your girlfriend stops sleeping with your best mate.'

It was a funny joke and it should have made her laugh out loud but instead she felt like crying. She blinked a couple of times and forced a smile. 'I'm really going to miss Popeye. Do you think I could—?' She looked at his shirt collar instead. 'No, maybe not. I'm not very good at goodbyes.'

'What time do you leave?' The question was as casual as *What do you think of the weather?*

'Early. It's a long drive.' Izzy was still focusing her gaze on his collar but it had become blurry. 'I don't want to rush it.'

'Izzy…' His throat moved up and down as if he had taken a bigger than normal swallow.

She looked into his grey-blue eyes, her heart feeling like it had moved out of her chest and was now beating in her oesophagus. 'Yes?'

His eyes moved back and forth between each of hers as if he was searching for something hidden there. 'Thank you for what you did for my father.'

Izzy wondered if that was what he had really intended to say. There was something about his tone and his manner that didn't seem quite right. 'I didn't do anything.'

He stopped dancing and stood with his arms still

around her, his eyes locked on hers. It was as if he had completely forgotten they were in the middle of the community centre dance floor, with the whole town watching on the sidelines. 'You didn't give up on him.'

Izzy gave him another wry smile. 'I like to give everyone a decent chance.'

He looked about to say something else but the jostling of the other dancers seemed to jolt him back into the present. A shutter came down on his face and he spoke in a flat monotone. 'We're holding up traffic.' He dropped his hands from her and stepped back. 'I'll let you mingle. I'll catch you later.'

'Zach…?' Izzy's voice was so husky it didn't stand a chance over the loud floor-stomping music Bill Davidson had exchanged for the ballad. She watched as Zach walked out of the community centre without even acknowledging Damien Redbank, who spoke to him on the way past.

It was another hour before Izzy could get anywhere near Zach again. She got caught up in a progressive barn dance and then a vigorous Scottish dance that left one of the older locals a little short of breath. She had to make sure the man was not having a cardiac arrest before she could go in search of Zach. She found him talking on his mobile out by the tank stand. He acknowledged her with a brief flicker of his lips as he slipped his phone away. 'All danced out?'

Izzy grimaced as she tucked a damp strand of hair behind her ear. 'I've been swung about so energetically I think both my shoulders have popped out of their sockets.'

'The Gay Gordons not your thing, then?' It was difficult to tell if he was smiling or not as his face was now in shadow.

'I loved it. It's the best workout I've had since…well, since last night.'

He stepped out of the cloaking shadow of the community centre but didn't look at her; instead, he was looking out into the sprawling endless darkness beyond town. 'That was my mother on the phone.'

'Does she call you often?'

'Not often.' Izzy heard him scrape the gravel with the toe of his boot. 'That's probably as much my fault as hers.'

'Would you ever consider going over to see her again some time?'

He lifted a shoulder and then let it drop. 'Maybe.'

'Maybe you could look me up if you do.' As soon as she'd said the words she wished she hadn't. They made her sound as if she was content to be nothing more than a booty call. She wanted more. *So much more.*

'What would be the point?'

Izzy rolled her lips together. 'It would be nice to catch up.'

'To do what?' His eyes looked as hard as diamond chips now. 'To pick up where we left off?'

She let out a slow, measured breath. 'I just thought—'

'What did you think, Izzy?' His tone hardened, along with his gaze. 'That I'd ask you to hang around so we could pretend a little longer this is going to last for ever? This was never about for ever. We've had our fun. Now it's time for you to leave as planned.'

Izzy swallowed a knot of pain. 'Is that what you want?'

His expression went back to its fall-back position. Distant. Aloof. Closed off. 'Of course it is.'

'I don't believe you.' She held his strong gaze with indomitable force. 'You're lying. You want me to stay. I know you do. You *want* me, Zach. I feel it in every fibre of my being. How can you stand there and pretend you don't?'

His mouth flattened. 'Don't make this ugly, Izzy.'

'You're the one making it ugly,' she said. 'You're making out that what we've shared has been nothing more than some tawdry little affair. How can you do that?'

A pulse beat like a hammer in his jaw. 'It was good sex. But I can have that with anyone. So can you.'

Izzy looked at him in wounded shock. This was not how things were supposed to be. The flag of hope in her chest was slipping back down the flagpole in despair. It was strangling her. Choking her. He was supposed to tell her he wanted more time with her. That he wanted her to stay. That he loved her. Not tell her she was replaceable.

Somehow she garnered her pride. 'Fine. Let's do it your way, then.' She stuck out her hand. 'Goodbye, Zach.'

He ignored her hand. He stood looking down at her with a stony expression on his face as if everything inside him had turned to marble. He didn't even speak. Not one word. Even the ticking pulse in his jaw had stopped.

Izzy returned her hand to her side. She would not let him see how much she was hurting. She straightened her shoulders and put one foot in front of the other as she walked back to the lights and music of the community centre.

When she got to the door and glanced back he was nowhere to be seen.

'All packed?' Margie asked, her smile sad and her eyes watery, as Izzy was about to head off the next morning.

'All packed.' Izzy had covered the track marks of her tears with the clever use of make-up but she wasn't sure the camouflage was going to last too long. Fresh tears were pricking like needles at the backs of her eyes and her heart felt like it was cracking into pieces. She'd lain awake most of the night, hoping Zach would come to her and tell her he'd made a terrible mistake, that he wanted her to stay, that he loved her with a for-ever love. But he hadn't turned up. He hadn't even sent a text. But that was his way. She had only known him four weeks but she knew that much about him. Once his mind was made up that was it. Over and out. No going back.

Doug shuffled forward to envelop her in a hug. 'Thanks.'

Izzy knew how much emotion was in that one simple word. She felt it vibrating in his body as she hugged him back as if he too was trying not to cry. 'Take care of yourself.'

'Where's Zach?' Margie asked Doug. 'I thought he'd be here to say goodbye.'

Doug's expression showed his frustration. 'I haven't seen him since daylight. Didn't say a word to me other than grunting something about taking Popeye for a walk. Haven't seen him since.'

'But I thought—' Margie began.

'He said all that needed to be said last night,' Izzy said, keeping her expression masked.

'Should've been here to see you off,' Doug said, frowning. 'What's got into him?'

Margie gave him a cautioning look before reaching to hug Izzy. 'I'm going to miss you *so* much.'

'I'll miss you too.'

With one last hug apiece Izzy got into her car and drove out of town. She had to blink to clear her vision as an overwhelming tide of emotion welled up inside her; it felt like she was leaving a part of herself behind.

She was.

Her heart.

Zach skimmed a stone across the surface of Blake's waterhole, watching as it skipped across the water six times before sinking. His record was fourteen skips but he wasn't getting anywhere near that today. He had been out here since dawn, trying to make sense of his feelings after his decision last night to end things with Izzy.

He kept reminding himself it was better this way. A clean cut healed faster than a festering sore.

But it didn't feel better. It felt worse. It hurt to think of Izzy driving away to her next post, finding some other guy to spend the rest of her life with while he tried to get on with his life out here.

He had never been a big believer in love at first sight. He had shied away from it because of what had happened between his parents. They'd married after a whirlwind courtship and his mother had spent the next decade being miserable and taking it out on everyone around her.

He didn't want to do that to Izzy. She hadn't had

enough time to get to know herself outside a relationship. He had no right to ask her to stay. What if she ended up hating him for it after a few weeks, months or years down the track?

He skimmed another stone but it only managed four skips before sinking. It felt like his heart, plummeting to the depths where it would never find the light of day again.

He thought of Izzy's smile, the way it lit up her face, the way it had beamed upon the dark sadness he had buried inside himself all those years ago. Would anyone else make him feel that spreading warmth inside his chest? Would anyone else make him feel alive and hopeful in spite of all the sickness and depravity of humanity he had to deal with in his work?

Izzy was not just a ray of sunshine.

She was *his* light.

He'd wanted to tell her last night. He'd *ached* to tell her. The words had been there but he'd kept swallowing them back down with common sense.

She was young and idealistic, full of romantic notions that didn't always play out in the real world. He was cynical and older in years, not to mention experience.

How could they make it work? How did any relationship work? *Could* they make theirs work?

How could he let her leave without telling her what he felt about her? If she didn't feel the same, he would have to bear that. At least he would be honest with her. He owed her that.

He owed himself that.

Zach drove out to the highway with Popeye on the seat beside him. 'I can't believe I'm doing this.' Popeye gave an excited yap. 'I mean it's crazy. I never do things like this. We've only known each other a month. It's not like she said she loved me. Not outright. What if I've got this wrong? What if she says no?' His fingers gripped the steering-wheel so tightly he was reminded of his grip on the veranda rail all those years ago.

What would have happened if he'd called out to his mother that day? Would it have changed anything? If nothing else, at least it would have assured his mother he loved her, even if she'd still felt the need to leave. He had never told his mother he loved her. Not since he was a little kid. That was something he would have to fix.

But not right now.

Miraculously, he suddenly saw Izzy's car ahead. He forced himself to slow down and watched her for a while, mentally rehearsing what he was going to say. He wasn't good at expressing emotion. He had spent his childhood locking away what he'd felt. His job had reinforced that pattern, demanding he kept his emotions under control at all times and in all places. What if he couldn't say what he wanted to say? Should he just blurt it out or lead in to it? His stomach was in knots. His heart felt as if it was in danger of splitting right down the middle.

He loved her.

He *really* loved her.

Not the pedestrian feelings he'd felt for Naomi.

His love for Izzy was a once-in-a-lifetime love. An all-or-nothing love.

A grand passion.

A for-ever love.

He suddenly realised her car was gathering speed. He checked his radar monitor. She was going twenty kilometres per hour over the limit! Acting on autopilot, he reached for his siren and lights switch, all the bells and whistles blaring as he put his foot down on the throttle.

Izzy was reaching for another tissue when she heard a police siren behind her. She glanced in the rear-view mirror, her heart flipping like a pancake flung by a master chef when she saw Zach behind the wheel, bearing down on her. She put her foot on the brake and pulled over to the gravel verge, trying to wipe the smeared mascara away from beneath her eyes. If he wanted a cold, clean break then that's what she would give him. Cold and clinical.

His tall, commanding figure appeared at her driver's window. The rim of his police hat shadowed his eyes and his voice was all business. 'Want to tell me why you were going twenty over the limit?'

She pressed her lips together. So that was going to be his parting gift, was it? *A speeding ticket!* 'I'm sorry, Officer, but I was reaching for a tissue.'

'Why are you crying?'

'I'm *not* crying.'

'Get out of the car.'

Izzy glowered at him. 'What *is* this?'

'I said get out of the car.'

She blew her cheeks out on a breath and stepped out, throwing him a defiant look. 'See? I'm not crying.'

His gaze held hers with his inscrutable one. 'Either you've been crying or you put your make-up on in the dark.'

Izzy put her hands on her hips and stared him down. 'Is it a crime to feel a little sad about leaving a town

I've grown to love? Is it, Sergeant show-no-emotion Fletcher? If so, go ahead and book me.'

A tiny glint came into his eyes. 'You love Jerringa Ridge?'

She folded her arms across her chest, still keeping her defiant glare in place. 'Yes.'

'What do you love about it?'

She was starting to feel a flutter of hope inside her chest, like a butterfly coming out of a chrysalis. 'I love the way it made me feel like I was the most beautiful person in the world. I love the way it made me feel passion I've never felt before. I love the way it opened its arms to me and held me close and made me feel safe.'

'That all?'

'That about covers it.'

He gave a slow nod. 'So...Brisbane, huh?'

She kept her chin up. 'Yes.'

He took off his hat and put it on the roof of her car, his movements slow, measured. 'You looking forward to that?'

'Not particularly.'

'Why not?'

Izzy looked into his now twinkling eyes. 'Because I'd much rather be here with you.'

He put his arms around her then, holding her so tightly against him she felt every button on his shirt pressing into her skin. 'I love you,' he said. 'I should've told you last night. I almost did...but I didn't want to put any pressure on you to stay. A public proposal seemed... I don't know...kind of tacky. Kind of manipulative.'

She looked up into his face with a wide-eyed look. 'A proposal?'

His expression was suddenly serious again. 'Izzy,

darling, I know we've only known each other a month. I know you have a life back in England, family and friends and roots that go deep. I would never ask you to give any of that up. All I'm asking is for you to give us a chance. We can make our home wherever you want to be. I can employ a manager for Fletcher Downs. Dad and Margie will be able to keep an eye on things. We can have the best of both worlds.' He cupped her face in his hands. '*You* are my world, darling girl. Marry me?'

Izzy smiled the widest smile she had ever smiled. 'Yes.'

He looked shocked. Taken aback. '*Yes?*'

'Yes, Zach.' She gave a little laugh at his expression. 'I will marry you. Why are you looking so surprised?'

'Because I didn't think it was possible to find some-one like you.' He stroked her hair back from her face, his expression tender. 'Someone who would make me feel like this. I didn't know it could happen so fast and so completely. I want to spend the rest of my life with you. I think a part of me realised that the first time we kissed. It scared the hell out of me, to tell you the truth.'

'I felt that way too,' Izzy said. 'I was so miserable last night. I couldn't believe you were just going to leave it at that after all we'd shared. Our relationship was supposed to be a fling but nothing about it felt like a fling to me.'

He hugged her tightly again. 'I was trying to do the right thing by you by letting you go. But I couldn't be-lieve how the right thing felt so incredibly painful. I decided I had to tell you how I felt, otherwise I'd spend the rest of my life regretting it.'

Her eyes twinkled as she looked up to hold his gaze. 'Promise me something?'

'Anything.'

'No five-star destinations for our honeymoon, OK?'

His eyes glinted again. 'You want to go camping?'

'Yes, and I want to swim naked and make love under the stars.' She hugged him close. 'I don't even mind if Max comes along as long as he has his own tent.'

'No way, baby girl,' Zach said. 'Max will have to find another place to stay while we're on our honeymoon. I'm not sharing you with anyone. Where is he, by the way?'

She gave him a sheepish look. 'He's in the boot. He wasn't too happy about being stashed in there but your dad and Margie came to say goodbye and I didn't have time to let him down properly.'

Zach grinned at her and pulled her close again. 'Maybe if I kiss you right now I won't think I'm dreaming this is happening. What do you reckon?'

She smiled as his mouth came down towards hers. 'I think that's an excellent idea.'

* * * * *

Mills & Boon® Hardback
April 2014

ROMANCE

A D'Angelo Like No Other	Carole Mortimer
Seduced by the Sultan	Sharon Kendrick
When Christakos Meets His Match	Abby Green
The Purest of Diamonds?	Susan Stephens
Secrets of a Bollywood Marriage	Susanna Carr
What the Greek's Money Can't Buy	Maya Blake
The Last Prince of Dahaar	Tara Pammi
The Sicilian's Unexpected Duty	Michelle Smart
One Night with Her Ex	Lucy King
The Secret Ingredient	Nina Harrington
Her Soldier Protector	Soraya Lane
Stolen Kiss From a Prince	Teresa Carpenter
Behind the Film Star's Smile	Kate Hardy
The Return of Mrs Jones	Jessica Gilmore
Her Client from Hell	Louisa George
Flirting with the Forbidden	Joss Wood
The Last Temptation of Dr Dalton	Robin Gianna
Resisting Her Rebel Hero	Lucy Ryder

MEDICAL

200 Harley Street: Surgeon in a Tux	Carol Marinelli
200 Harley Street: Girl from the Red Carpet	Scarlet Wilson
Flirting with the Socialite Doc	Melanie Milburne
His Diamond Like No Other	Lucy Clark

Mills & Boon® Large Print
April 2014

ROMANCE

Defiant in the Desert	Sharon Kendrick
Not Just the Boss's Plaything	Caitlin Crews
Rumours on the Red Carpet	Carole Mortimer
The Change in Di Navarra's Plan	Lynn Raye Harris
The Prince She Never Knew	Kate Hewitt
His Ultimate Prize	Maya Blake
More than a Convenient Marriage?	Dani Collins
Second Chance with Her Soldier	Barbara Hannay
Snowed in with the Billionaire	Caroline Anderson
Christmas at the Castle	Marion Lennox
Beware of the Boss	Leah Ashton

HISTORICAL

Not Just a Wallflower	Carole Mortimer
Courted by the Captain	Anne Herries
Running from Scandal	Amanda McCabe
The Knight's Fugitive Lady	Meriel Fuller
Falling for the Highland Rogue	Ann Lethbridge

MEDICAL

Gold Coast Angels: A Doctor's Redemption	Marion Lennox
Gold Coast Angels: Two Tiny Heartbeats	Fiona McArthur
Christmas Magic in Heatherdale	Abigail Gordon
The Motherhood Mix-Up	Jennifer Taylor
The Secret Between Them	Lucy Clark
Craving Her Rough Diamond Doc	Amalie Berlin

0314 GEN STD LP

Mills & Boon® Hardback
May 2014

ROMANCE

The Only Woman to Defy Him	Carol Marinelli
Secrets of a Ruthless Tycoon	Cathy Williams
Gambling with the Crown	Lynn Raye Harris
The Forbidden Touch of Sanguardo	Julia James
One Night to Risk it All	Maisey Yates
A Clash with Cannavaro	Elizabeth Power
The Truth About De Campo	Jennifer Hayward
Sheikh's Scandal	Lucy Monroe
Beach Bar Baby	Heidi Rice
Sex, Lies & Her Impossible Boss	Jennifer Rae
Lessons in Rule-Breaking	Christy McKellen
Twelve Hours of Temptation	Shoma Narayanan
Expecting the Prince's Baby	Rebecca Winters
The Millionaire's Homecoming	Cara Colter
The Heir of the Castle	Scarlet Wilson
Swept Away by the Tycoon	Barbara Wallace
Return of Dr Maguire	Judy Campbell
Heatherdale's Shy Nurse	Abigail Gordon

MEDICAL

200 Harley Street: The Proud Italian	Alison Roberts
200 Harley Street: American Surgeon in London	Lynne Marshall
A Mother's Secret	Scarlet Wilson
Saving His Little Miracle	Jennifer Taylor

0414GEN STD HB

Mills & Boon® Large Print
May 2014

ROMANCE

The Dimitrakos Proposition	Lynne Graham
His Temporary Mistress	Cathy Williams
A Man Without Mercy	Miranda Lee
The Flaw in His Diamond	Susan Stephens
Forged in the Desert Heat	Maisey Yates
The Tycoon's Delicious Distraction	Maggie Cox
A Deal with Benefits	Susanna Carr
Mr (Not Quite) Perfect	Jessica Hart
English Girl in New York	Scarlet Wilson
The Greek's Tiny Miracle	Rebecca Winters
The Final Falcon Says I Do	Lucy Gordon

HISTORICAL

From Ruin to Riches	Louise Allen
Protected by the Major	Anne Herries
Secrets of a Gentleman Escort	Bronwyn Scott
Unveiling Lady Clare	Carol Townend
A Marriage of Notoriety	Diane Gaston

MEDICAL

Gold Coast Angels: Bundle of Trouble	Fiona Lowe
Gold Coast Angels: How to Resist Temptation	Amy Andrews
Her Firefighter Under the Mistletoe	Scarlet Wilson
Snowbound with Dr Delectable	Susan Carlisle
Her Real Family Christmas	Kate Hardy
Christmas Eve Delivery	Connie Cox

0414 GEN STD LP

Discover more romance at

www.millsandboon.co.uk

- ❤ WIN great prizes in our exclusive competitions

- ❤ BUY new titles before they hit the shops

- ❤ BROWSE new books and REVIEW your favourites

- ❤ SAVE on new books with the Mills & Boon® Bookclub™

- ❤ DISCOVER new authors

PLUS, to chat about your favourite reads, get the latest news and find special offers:

- Find us on facebook.com/millsandboon
- Follow us on twitter.com/millsandboonuk
- ❤ Sign up to our newsletter at millsandboon.co.uk